# THE DARK BELOW THE ICE

# AND OTHER STORIES

Kenton J Moore

The Dark Below the Ice: and Other Stories

Copyright © 2023 Kenton J Moore

Published in Canada by Soulforge Media

Cover Design and Interior Design by Kenton Moore



This is a work of fiction. Names, characters, businesses,
events and incidents are the products of the author's
imagination. Any resemblance to actual persons, living or
dead, or actual events is purely coincidental.

ISBN:

978-1-7770866-6-4  (Soft-cover edition)

978-1-7770866-7-1  (E-book edition)

Printing and distribution in Soft Cover, and E-Book by
IngramSpark, USA.

I dedicate this collection to everyone who ever told me
to keep going. To every friend, family member, and fan
who wouldn't let me quit.

And to my Mom, who was the loudest voice of them all.

## FOREWORD

If you were to ask me what I enjoy writing most, out of all the genres and sub-genres in the literary world, I would have to say it is what you will find in the pages of this collection. Of all my written work, I enjoy mystery, thrillers, horror, and suspense the most. My favourite type of story to experience, and therefore to write, is one where you spend the entire story certain of some incredible supernatural power, only to discover subtle hints that it never was. I love deep narrative, where discussion breeds like rats among people trying to pull at the tapestry of truth woven in our words. I like a story that makes you think, and question, what is real or what could be.

As I grew both as a person and as a writer, I discovered the ability to understand my emotional reactions to life through my writing. I learned to deal with loss, death, fear, surprise, and nightmares through my stories. Fear especially. I learned to turn the things that scared me the most in life into stories, and thus I found myself no longer afraid of those things.

I think that started with my Mother when I was younger. I'd watched a scary movie and woke from nightmares about it. I remember Mom telling me "It's just make-believe, it can't hurt you." And so I learned to trap my fears in the make-believe. To weave the darkness into a comfy blanket I could sleep under in the light.

You will see this as you read through the stories in this collection. From my fear of a time I fell through the ice on the Thompson River taking center stage in the title story The Dark Below the Ice, to my Bathophobia in the Navy showing up in Seven Turns of the Screw. Even the very real and very modern fear of cancel culture appears in the Last Post story.

Not all the stories herein were birthed in that way for me. The Engineer's Nightmare came from a desire to explore the history of my favourite character in my Magnum Opus Steampunk novels (coming soon). The Journey was the result of a challenge set forth by my good friend Jen when she sent me a random picture and told me to write a 2,000-word story on it for practice. The First was the result of inspiration and isolation after finishing an incredible novel a friend wrote while I was in Ontario on a military training course.

Regardless of the origin of the story, this collection contains twelve of my favourite dark stories that I have written over the years. Some of these works, my closest friends and family might have read before. Most of them have never been seen. Never been shared. I hope you enjoy them. Welcome to the shadow of my mind. Welcome, to the Dark Below the Ice.

# TABLE OF CONTENTS


The First ............................................. pg. 9

The Dark Below the Ice ................... pg. 35

NecRomantic .................................... pg. 70

The Taste of Tears .......................... pg. 81

The Touch of Shadow ...................... pg. 98

Seven Turns of the Screw ............. pg. 109

The Journey ..................................... pg. 127

The Engineer's Nightmare ............. pg. 136

The Last Post ................................... pg. 142

PACO ................................................. pg. 157

Emergence ....................................... pg. 162

The Haunting of
Old Man Ritter ................................. pg. 177

8

# THE FIRST

It was the smell of the blood that got to me. Metallic yet somehow stale, almost like the horrible smell frying liver made back when Mom cooked it for me all the time. My left hand instinctively cupped under my nose, as my right lifted the yellow Police Line tape so I could duck under it. The front door of the house opened into an open-concept living room with a stairway to the left which led upstairs. Detective Rainier Tremblay held out a small jar of Vapo-Rub as I approached, retrieving his pen from his pocket after I accepted the cream. My eyes followed his briefing around the details of the room as I dabbed some Vapo-Rub on my finger and applied it to my upper lip. Sure it made my eyes run, but it did wonders for the smell.

"Two victims. Adult female, age 37, stabbed

numerous times," I followed Tremblay's pointing pen to my right where I could make out the mangled remains of a blonde-haired woman lying awkwardly between the couch and a glass coffee table. The Medical Examiners and CSI Photographers were crawling all over the scene, cataloguing every shred of evidence they could find, while yet more personnel analyzed the spray patterns of the blood all over the room; and I meant all over the room.

"What a mess…" I whispered, interrupting Tremblay's briefing. Tremblay simply looked at me and shrugged.

"One point five gallons in the human body… I'd bet she has little left in there."

One point five gallons. The room looked as though a third-year fine art student high as hell on whatever mind-bending drug is cool these days had turned the space into some kind of statement on the way our consumerism is destroying the planet. And that smell. Even through the Vapo-Rub, it was enough for me to have to consciously focus on not gagging. Red ran in streaking arcs across the floor, the walls, and even in spots across the ceiling. Yellow evidence photography tags were everywhere.

The medical examiner standing over the victim stood and shook his head. Even with all his protective equipment on, I recognized him right away. He looked over at Tremblay and me as he wiped the sweat from his forehead with the back of his wrist. I liked him. He always managed to see things we missed. He would always joke about it being because he's Asian. Called it his "Asian racial bonus." Plus two to math and sciences. I had no idea what the hell he was talking about, but I liked him anyway.

"I count nineteen stab wounds to the torso and neck. Won't know for sure how many more there are everywhere else until we get her back to the morgue and clean all this blood off."

"Good work," I began. "We'll finish our sweep and then release the crime scene. Have the coroner get ready to move her."

I was just going through the motions. The scene was so grisly; I would have loved to authorize the coroners to move her right away. It almost felt like I would be doing the deceased a courtesy. No one deserves to have their life cut short. Especially like this. I looked at Tremblay, and his eyes met mine in a wordless request to continue with his briefing. I nodded and followed him across the living room floor past the art nouveau blood installation and into the kitchen area at the back end of the floor. A large marble-topped island separated the living area from the tiled kitchen. There was blood here too, though in smaller spatters and mostly centred around a huge chef's knife that lay on the tile near the fridge. The knife was of a single metal construction wherein the handle was moulded directly into the blade. At the base of the blade was a stamp that showed three prongs like those on a trident. It looked expensive, even though it was coated in blood and the tip had broken off.

"This is where we found the father. He was nearly catatonic, and didn't respond to questions or stimuli in any way."

"Drugs?" I asked, taking my pen out of my pocket as I lowered to a squat. I moved the evidence photography tag that was casting a shadow on the broken tip of the knife.

"Don't know yet. They're running toxicology on his blood."

"Where is he now?"

"Back at the station. He didn't put up any fight at all. It was like he wasn't even here; you know?"

I tapped the end of my pen lightly against the floor for a moment, pondering the angle of the knife and the bloody handprints on the counter to my right. I pictured for a moment how the man had leaned against the counter before collapsing to his knees and dropping the knife to his side. I motioned to the broken tip with my pen before I stood.

"Do we know where that broken piece is?"

Tremblay nodded, and his jaw set for a moment. He sighed as if he didn't want to say what came next.

"M.E. thinks it's inside the second victim. Lodged in her sternum."

"Her? Another woman?"

"His daughter. Upstairs. Seven years old."

My heart leapt into my throat. I hated murder cases involving children more than anything else in the world, and Tremblay knew it. I suddenly realized why we had started downstairs, and why he had left out the second victim right from the outset.

"Nick… you don't have to…" Tremblay began, knowing the raging fire that was going on inside me. I pushed past him before he could bring up her name, or anything about her.

"Yes, I do. It's my job. Show me."

Nick lowered his head and let me pass the kitchen island before following me back into the living room. Just before rounding the right-hand corner to begin climbing the stairs to the second floor, I hesitated. Tremblay moved past me and put his left foot up onto the first stair. He stopped and looked back at me, his eyes stern yet sympathetic.

"Are you sure, Nick? It's like Le Diable's playground up there…"

Without saying a word, I gestured with my pen for him to continue. Tremblay wasn't lying about his reference to the devil. I could feel my skin crawling more and more with every footfall up those stairs. The hair on the back of my neck stood up and sweat beaded on my forehead. I really had no idea what I would see, but at the moment I was focused on what I could feel. There was something ominous about the climb to the second floor, and even more so on the landing at the top. A presence was there, dark and terrifying, yet beyond my understanding. When we reached the end of the narrow hall, and Tremblay stood to the side of the door leading to the scene of the second victim's death, it took every ounce of courage I had to move past him and into the little girl's room.

Two things happened when that scene unfolded

before me. One, I suddenly believed in the devil. And two, I added a half-digested pumpkin spice latte and an apple fritter to the fluid collection the medical examiners would be forced to perform. The darkness I felt was palpable. I could have cut it with a knife. I had been on the force for close to eighteen years, awarded twice for professional conduct, but the absolute depravity I saw before me was enough to chuck my cookies once more back out in the hallway while Tremblay desperately tried to return from the upstairs bathroom with some paper towel.

"Tabarnak esti…" Tremblay said, allowing some of his rarely used Quebecois show. "I warned you."

I slowly came to my senses and the world stopped spinning. Wiping the vomit from my mouth had also removed my thin layer of protection from the horrid smell of all the blood, so the first thing I did was retrieve the Vapo-Rub from my pocket and apply a fresh liberal coat. I sniffed deeply, allowing the vapour to expunge all the horror from my sinus, and then stood. I coughed a little, ensuring that the upset in my stomach was over. For now.

"Eighteen years, Rainier. Eighteen years and I never chucked biscuits on a crime scene. Please tell me forensics has been up here already."

I could tell Tremblay wanted to laugh, and a huge part of me wished he would, but instead, he simply ushered me back toward the stairs. I had no desire to go back into that room. What I saw would already be with me for the remainder of my days.

"They have. We were just waiting on your sweep

to clear the scene."

When we reached the bottom of the stairs, my favourite Asian medical examiner was waiting for us, his goggles now hanging around his neck and his gloves removed. He looked at me inquisitively.

"Clear it. We're done here."

As he moved to give the coroner's instructions, I reached out and grabbed him by the shoulder. He turned around and our eyes met. He had a faint smile, and I'm sure he knew already, but I told him anyway.

"I ralphed up there… sorry."

He shrugged and patted me on the ribs under my outstretched arm that rested on his shoulder.

"Hey… we can't all be perfect. Nice to know you're human."

I nodded and ducked under the tape that Tremblay was holding up for me. We walked silently down the concrete path that led up to the front door of the house. On the sidewalk, I stopped and turned to watch the beehive of activity as the crews prepared to clear the scene. The flashing lights from at least a half-dozen various emergency vehicles lit the house with an odd almost festive glow of colours. From the outside, the house looked so incredibly sterile. Hanging pots, well-tended gardens on both sides of the stairs up to the porch, a pink bike with training wheels and tassels dangling from the handles. I shivered, and for a moment, allowed myself to be mesmerized by the way those tassels reflected all the emergency lights. Then I turned to Tremblay.

"Okay… what the actual fuck goes through someone's mind to do…" I paused a moment, waving my hand in the air in circles as I tried to find a word. Finally, I simply motioned to the house. "…that!"

Tremblay shook his head. I could tell he had no more ideas than I did.

"It's crazy…" Tremblay began as he walked around to the driver's side of our unmarked squad car. "None of it makes any sense. Father loses it, completely butchers his wife and daughter, and then just… shuts down. Why didn't he touch the boy? That's what I don't get."

"The boy?" I asked as I opened the passenger door and slid into the seat. Tremblay slid behind the wheel and adjusted the seat. He was taller than me, after all, and I had been driving last since I arrived after him.

"Responders found a five-year-old boy just sitting on the stairs when they arrived. Untouched. Totally clean."

"Related to the perp?" I already suspected the answer, but Tremblay indulged me as he turned the car's ignition and dropped the transmission lever into drive.

"His son."

*******

For one o'clock in the morning, the precinct was unusually abuzz when Tremblay and I arrived.

Captain Turay came out of her office to greet us. She was wearing plain clothes and her jet-black curly hair was down in messy tangles. She was small in stature but made up for it with pure African-Canadian fury. Most of the men in the precinct called her Storm, after a comic book character. I didn't care where the name came from, because the moniker fit. She was a hurricane in her own right. Canting her hips to the side and resting her left hand on her waist, she gestured at me with her right hand, her coffee almost sloshing over the rim of her cup as she did.

"Nick… please tell me you didn't really heave your guts on a crime scene? And twice to boot? What's witchoo, boy?" She chided, the last part of her sentence accented with as much ghetto as she dared. She was still Chief of Police after all.

"Fuuuuck…" I breathed, shaking my head in shame. "That made it here already, did it?"

"Mmm-hmmm. Kristoff called it in."

"Remind me to shave-bomb his locker…"

The Chief looked me up and down and spun away back toward her office. Tremblay and I followed.

"I didn't hear that," she began as she rounded her desk and sat down. Tremblay and I took seats opposite her. "He's off shift until tomorrow. Eighteen hundred hours. You didn't hear that!"

Tremblay and I shared a glance and shrugged.

"Hear what?" we said, almost in tandem.

Her point made, Captain Turay shook her finger in the air and took a sip of coffee.

"Helluva night out there. What we got?"

"Two dead. Adult female, thirty-seven years of age. Female child, approximately seven years of age. Both stabbed. A lot. Father is in custody, almost catatonic. A five-year-old boy in the hands of child services, but found on the scene. We may need him for questioning. "

I was grateful for Tremblay taking the lead on this one. He was an excellent partner. I made a mental note to buy him a bottle of his favourite champagne to share with his wife. Captain Turay shot me a sympathetic glance.

"You need to speak to mental health about what happened tonight?"

The question caught me off guard. Made me realize I had spaced out for a few moments.

"What? No… I'm good, Captain. Locked and loaded."

Captain Turay nodded slowly, her words came slow and at low volume, but I could hear the tone of caring they carried.

"Locked and loaded…" she sat back in her chair and appraised the both of us, taking another sip of her coffee. "I want the child left in the hands of social services. Don't touch him unless you get nothing from the father, clear?"

We both nodded again.

"Alright. Let's put this to bed. Perp's in interrogation three, if you boys are up to it?"

I looked at Tremblay and saw the resolve burning in his eyes. He never took his eyes off the Captain.

Something in that look in his eyes told me he would forsake days of sleep if it meant closing this case. After what I had seen, I was right there with him. No words were spoken by either of us when I looked back at the Captain, but I could see the same look in her eyes as well.

"I'm going to need more coffee…" she sighed.

********

There was something completely unsettling about Thomas Barrow when Tremblay and I walked into interrogation room three. He sat completely motionless in the chair, arms draped at his sides with his cuffed wrists laid in his lap. His back was hunched over ever so slightly forward, and his head lowered to the point where his chin almost touched his chest. He very well could have appeared asleep were it not for his eyes. The haunting emptiness in their glazed stare was unnerving and gave the room a palpable chill.

"Thomas Barrow," Tremblay began, dropping the case file down on the desk with a thud. He was playing bad cop, and I was thankful for it. This whole case gave me the creeps. "Do you know where you are? You've been arrested for the murder of your wife and daughter…"

The mention of the daughter brought a shudder to my already aching muscles. My stomach threatened to upend, but I suppressed it as little more than a hiccup. Tremblay paused long enough to ensure I was okay, as he paced the room behind Thomas.

"You were found at the scene, the murder weapon right beside you, covered in their blood. I have to say… it's not looking good for you Mister Barrow. If I were you, I would tell us everything we need to know. And fast."

"Mister Barrow," I began, allowing myself to fall into the routine Tremblay and I had perfected over our years together on the force. I sat down in the chair opposite Thomas. "Please. We need to understand what happened this evening. Can you tell us, Mister Barrow? Tell us what happened tonight at your home?"

Thomas Barrow did something then that made my blood run like ice water through my veins. He twitched a single spastic jerk, and dark black blood began oozing from his ears and down his jawline in thin rivulets. His jet-black hair seemed almost alive.

"I killed the girl…" he spoke quietly, his voice strained and broken, like someone who had been screaming for days at a rock and roll festival. "With the kitchen knife. Stab, stab, stab… then the woman. She ran. I chased. Downstairs I caught her. Stab, stab, stab, stab…"

"Calisse tabarnak!!" Tremblay exclaimed as he backed against the wall. I shoved my chair back from the table and leapt to my feet. Thomas Barrow continued to repeat the word stab over and over in that grating, broken voice of his. The blood from his ears was a river now, joined by tendrils from the tear ducts of his eyes and a free flow from his nose. Suddenly, he simply stopped and opened his mouth. Grey-brown vomit rolled out unceremoniously and slid down the front of his shirt. There was nothing else.

I had no idea how much time had passed in silence as Tremblay and I stood in paralyzed fear, but it was the sound of the door busting open that made us both jump and shout. Captain Turay was there, along with two beat officers I didn't recognize and my medical examiner friend.

"What in the actual fuck just happened…" Captain Turay said, jabbing her finger at Thomas. "Check if that man is alive!"

The medical examiner stepped forward and pulled a surgical glove from his belt pouch first aid kit. He pulled the glove on with a snap and placed his index and middle fingers against Thomas' neck. The head shake he gave told us all we needed to know. Something had just killed Thomas in front of our eyes. Something none of us had ever seen before. Some new drug, perhaps. I looked over at Tremblay, who was still backed against the wall and staring at Thomas.

"We didn't…" my words failed me, and my voice just seemed to trail off. Captain Turay spoke next, and suddenly I realized she had been watching from behind the two-way the whole time.

"I know, Nick. We were just on our way in to tell you the latest."

Tremblay seemed to snap out of his trance and

looked from Captain Turay to the medical examiner and back.

"We?"

"Toxicology came back from the labs," the medical examiner began. "And that's where things got really weird."

"Weirder than this?" I almost shouted, motioning to the corpse of Thomas Barrow.

"According to our toxicology reports… this man died nearly six hours ago."

"Impossible!" I barked. "That's before we even got the call!"

The medical examiner shrugged.

"Blood samples taken at time of arrest to test for drugs showed his blood already congealed."

"Okay, enough…" Captain Turay began. She turned to the examiner. "Get him out of here. I want a full autopsy ASAP." She turned to Tremblay, and then to me. "This is some spooky shit."

I nodded my agreement and leaned back against the two-way glass. I felt like the Captain at that moment, had a real penchant for understatement.

"What do we do?" Asked Tremblay as he watched the examiner and the beat cop go to work bagging the body. Captain Turay ran her hands through her hair, then looked down at the medical examiner.

"Any chance whatever's going on is some infectious shit? Some… I dunno…"

"You mean like zombies?" The examiner asked.

"Yes. Like zombies." Turay was out of her

element. I could see that. Hell… we all were.

"No," the examiner scoffed. "Tox was clean beyond the congealing."

Captain Turay thought for a long moment before turning to face me. She was close, I could smell her late-night sweat mixed with coffee breath. Still better than that house.

"We need answers here. Fast."

She paused a moment, tapping her finger against her chin before shoving that same finger into my chest.

"Bring in the boy. No matter what it takes."

I nodded and she turned and walked out of the room, following the body bag being carried by the examiner and one of the beat cops. I turned to look at Tremblay, who was staring at the chair Thomas had sat in. Black blood and specks of the grey-brown vomit dotted the chair. We both gagged and bolted from the room.

*********

By the time we were ready to bring in the boy, the entire goddamn province was all over the story. Word had spread like wildfire about a white-picket-fence man living the Canadian Dream who suddenly snapped and butchered his family, sparing a little boy, the case's sole lead. Due to the sudden prestige of the whole affair, we were given time to go home, rest, and shower. Shower, I did. For quite a long time, in fact, and accompanied by a straight bottle of whiskey.

Rest? That part not so much. The story was all over the news, and when I finally arrived back at the precinct for the interrogation, I had to make my way through a whole throng of reporters. Thank God, I thought, that none of them knew about the puke.

Inside the Captain's office, Tremblay leaned against the wall, arms crossed. He was unusually silent. Captain Turay paced back and forth. She was in her full dress uniform, probably because she was expected to make a statement following the interrogations. The media frenzy and all that. She looked up and gave me a sympathetic smile as I entered the room.

"The vultures outside didn't tear any meat from you, did they?"

I shook my head. I knew how to deal with the press.

Shortly after me, a tall blonde woman in a crisp business suit entered the room. Amy Ryanson. The district attorney. She was a livid bitch, almost impossible to please and way too happy to throw around threats. This kept getting worse and worse.

"Has the boy arrived?" Amy barked, her sultry voice masking the venom she always spewed.

Captain Turay shook her head, but before she could speak, Amy was barking again.

"Who is leading the interrogation?"

My throat caught when Captain Turay said my name. Amy turned on me, and I instinctively averted my eyes. She was like Medusa somehow; her gaze could make most men freeze. Not turn to stone, obviously, but freeze in other ways. She just had a way of de-powering people. I figure that's how she became district attorney in the first place. I knew what was coming next, and it made my blood boil.

"I want someone else on this. Detective Perega is not fit to conduct this investigation, and I don't think I need to explain why."

I could no longer keep my eyes away. The surprise that flooded through me brought a powerful wave of confidence, along with something else. Rage.

"Oh," I began, my voice barely hiding the fury building inside me. "I very much think you do need to explain, Amy."

"Very well," she began, as she moved towards me. She was catlike, full of posturing and bravado. She swayed her hips as though she was swishing her tail, readying to pounce, but my anger let me see right through her, and I was not backing down.

"You're too close to this. Too emotional. Do you really expect to successfully interrogate a child when only a year ago, you buried your own?"

There it was. I knew it. This bitch had been on my tail ever since our daughter's accident, trying in some way to prove that her 'useless detective ex-husband' was responsible for her death. She always went back to this. Always. I had simply had enough.

"Enough with this bullshit!" Captain Turay shouted.

Amy stopped inches from my face, and I could feel the hatred burning behind her sky-blue irises. She blamed me. She always would. I saw her lip quiver for just a moment; and saw a hint of moisture rim her eyes. I gritted my teeth so hard that I heard them squeak, and she heard it too.

"You two need to stow your shit, and stow it NOW!" Captain Turay hollered. "I got half the media in central Canada outside my precinct and I need my lead detective and our D.A. to do their bloody jobs!"

I didn't need to say a word. My eyes said it all, and after a long moment of testing each other's resolve, Amy backed down.

"Fine," Amy said as she barged out of the office. "Don't blame me if he fucks up again. I warned you."

Tremblay breathed a massive sigh of relief as I lowered my head and idly stroked my ring finger. It was Captain Turay who broke the ice.

"Suck it up, Nick," she said, her tone softer and sympathetic. "We know the truth, and you have a job to do."

As the Captain made her way around the desk and strode to the door, Nick and Tremblay fell in behind her.

"Don't know what the fuck you ever saw in that one, Nick…" Turay whispered under her breath.

I couldn't help but let a little smile creep onto the corner of my mouth as we all headed for the interrogation rooms.

*******

Nathan Barrow was just like any other five-year-old boy I'd ever met. He was pure innocence, sitting on the chair in the interrogation room playing with a toy train and police cruiser. He was smiling and upbeat, his short brown curly hair a pleasant mix of his Father's black and his Mother's blonde. The police cruiser was chasing the train and calling for the robbers to stop because they were under arrest for stealing a train. A representative from social services and a trauma counsellor stood toward the back of the room and near the door, whispering to one another and watching like hawks. I sat across from Nathan the way I had sat across from his father. The thought of Thomas made me shiver. Behind the glass, I knew that Amy, Tremblay, the Captain, and probably a host of others were watching intently, so I wasted as little time as I could.

"Hello, Nathan. My name is Nick."

"Hello!" Nathan cooed as the police cruiser finally managed to crash into the train, sending it flipping across the table to the astonishment of the robbers.

"Nathan, I need to ask you some questions. Do you think that would be okay?"

"Sure."

"Nathan…" I nervously glanced at the trauma counsellor and the social services rep. The trauma counsellor nodded that it was okay for me to proceed. "Nathan, something very bad happened yesterday, and I know you may be too scared to talk about it, but we need to understand what happened.

Can you tell me what happened when your Mom and Sister were hurt?"

I felt completely uneasy, and a wave of cold fear washed over me. How could I expect a five-year-old child to understand what I was asking of him? How would he have interpreted those horrific events in his growing mind? I glanced again at the trauma counsellor and saw no disagreement with the question.

"Daddy went through the breaking, and he killed Mommy and 'lizabeth."

My heart felt as though it had stopped in my chest. Whatever smoothness my skin had to it was now akin to the surface of the moon due to the goosebumps distorting my flesh. The temperature in the room felt suddenly arctic, and when I turned my head toward the mirror behind me and then to the counsellors, I could see I was not alone. Nathan had stopped playing and sat bolt upright, completely engaged and nonchalantly talking about his family's murder as though it were a game he was playing. Maybe it was.

"The breaking?" I squeaked, surprised at the frailty of my voice.

"Yes. Chadwick showed me how to do it. I can't do it yet… because I'm still alive… so Chadwick did it to Daddy to show me how it's done."

I swallowed hard, but my mouth and throat felt like ash. Five-year-old children have incredible imaginations; I knew that much. Especially after seeing the way he played out the scene with the train robbers and the police cruiser, but something about the sincere innocence he was portraying here was beyond terrifying.

"Can you tell me where we can find Chadwick?"

"Chadwick lives on the other side of the veil. He's kinda like a ghost? Only he's real because he talks to me."

At the mention of ghosts, I relaxed a little bit, even if this whole situation was something from the Twilight Zone.

"Could I talk to Chadwick, Nathan?"

Nathan shook his little head, thought for a moment, and then shrugged. It was the first normal thing the boy had done since the interrogation had begun.

"No… maybe… I dunno. It's hard for him to talk to me. He can only do it when he holds me in that spot between asleep and awake. Chadwick says that place is like a skin between us and the veil. Some people get trapped there when they die, and Chadwick knows how to use them. It's why we sometimes talk to people who have died in our dreams. Like Sandra."

This time I felt a palpable pain squeeze the inside of my chest. My heartbeat hammered in my ears, and my vision blurred. I knew it was because my eyes had become wet with tears.

"You miss her, don't you, Nick? Sandra Perega. Your daughter?"

At that moment, time slowed to a stop. I was vaguely aware of a muffled thump and some distant yelling from behind the mirror. It was all I could do but stare at the little boy sitting across from me. The little boy who when I had come in was such an innocent child playing with his toys. The little boy who had spoken of ghosts. The little boy who had spoken of my dead daughter.

The door blew open and I didn't take my eyes off the boy. Amy shot into the room like a ballistic missile headed straight for the boy and still, I didn't flinch. The counsellors tried to intercept her, but they collided with Captain Turay and Tremblay as they thundered into the room behind Amy. Still, the boy and I locked our eyes together, and my breath came in ragged pulls while he calmly looked back at me. Those innocent eyes. I heard his voice, though it was clear his lips weren't moving.

Do you want to see the breaking, Nick? Chadwick can show it to you.

Amy was viciously shaking Nathan and screaming, but it sounded like an echo in a public pool when you were underwater. Even as the boy was thrashed around by Amy, and the others tried desperately to pull her off of him, his eyes never left mine.

The breaking won't hurt, Nick. You could see Sandra again. Would you like that, Nick?

A single ice-cold tear rolled down my cheek and in that moment I heard a new voice inside my head as the world exploded around me.

"Close your eyes, Dad."

I did.

In the darkness, I saw a faint form take shape ever so slowly as if made by light and smoke. Like in a dream, I couldn't make out details, but I knew in my heart it was her. I felt peace and warmth wash over me like a hot shower after a cold winter run.

"Sandra…"

"Hi, Dad. Don't worry about me, okay? I'm fine. You need to stay away from that house. Stay away from that boy. Avoid the breaking, Dad… at all costs. Promise me."

"I promise. But… how is this even real?"

"I can't explain that, Dad. It just is."

"You're a ghost…"

"Yes."

"Does it hurt?"

Sandra laughed, a sweet sound filling my head like gentle chimes in a summer breeze.

"No. It doesn't hurt Dad. But I have to go now. You have to go."

"Why?"

"I don't have answers for you Dad."

"What is the breaking, Sandra?"

"Nothing good, Dad. Promise me you'll stay away."

"How will I stay away? So much has happened…"

"You'll know when you open your eyes."

"What does that mean?"

"Dad, I have to go. Promise me."

"Okay, Sandra… I promise I'll stay away.

"Thank you…"

"Sandra?"

"Yes?"

"I…""

"I know Dad. It's not your fault. I love you."

Then she was gone, and I was alone in the darkness behind my eyes. The comfort of her presence remained, however, and when I opened my eyes, I was standing in front of Thomas Barrow's house, once more in that moment before Tremblay and I had left. I blinked my eyes rapidly, trying to comprehend what had just happened. The festive emergency lights blinking against the walls, the strange eerie serenity of it all flooded in and I drew a deep breath. Part of me half expected to wake up suddenly inside the interrogation room again; where all hell had broken loose because of one strange boy and his ghost story. Instead, the air in my lungs carried the burning scent of Vapo-Rub and the faint odour of blood and vomit.

I was back before it all had happened. This was real. I caught a shimmer on the grass near the path; and let myself get lost in the reflections of those tassels on the pink bike again. Somehow, whatever Sandra had done had lifted a dreadful weight inside me. Maybe it was her assurance that her accident wasn't my fault. Maybe it was being put back before it all happened. Maybe it was everything all at once. Somehow, deep down inside me, I felt a spark. I felt a rebirth if such a thing was possible.

"It's crazy…" Tremblay began as he walked around to the driver's side of our unmarked squad car. "None of it makes any sense. Father loses it, completely butchers his wife and daughter, and then just... shuts down. Why didn't he touch the boy? That's what I don't get."

I let the events that had transpired wash over me in rapid succession. Thomas' interrogation, the media frenzy, the fight with Amy, Nathan, and Sandra. It couldn't have been a dream, could it? I knew it wasn't, but I had no explanations at all for how I knew. Something happened, whether it was Nathan, Chadwick, or Sandra, and I was back here again. At the beginning. Maybe I'll never know how or why... but I do know that somehow... someway... this was real. I sighed, taking one long look at the house.

"Hey..." Tremblay said from the other side of the car. "You okay, Nick?"

I turned and faced him; offered the best smile I could muster and hoped he didn't see through it.

"Yeah. I'm good. What did you say?"

"I said I don't get this. Why did the father lose it? And why spare the boy?"

"I don't know," I said as I opened the passenger door and slid into the seat. "I just know I don't want to touch this case with a ten-foot pole. We got the guy at the scene red-handed, no pun intended. Best to leave well enough alone. Let's call it in. File reports in the morning."

"You sure Turay will like that? The perps in the station waiting on interrogation..."

"I'll explain it. This one's on me. I have a feeling he won't mind waiting for someone else."

Tremblay shrugged and started the car and dropped the shift stick into drive.

"Crazy… man going nuts like that."

"Yeah," I said. "Crazy how some people just… break."


LA FIN

# THE DARK BELOW THE ICE

Annabelle Lewis stepped out onto her deck and drew a deep breath of the cold mountain air as she surveyed the frozen lake spread out beyond her. The moonlit sky cast an otherworldly glow on the bare ice, reflecting only in the cracks and impurities of the surface. To say that it looked as smooth as glass did not do the scene justice, it was more as though the lake was a broken mirror in a dark attic, laying peacefully below peaked mountains not yet shed of their snow. Annabelle ran her hand through her medium-length white hair, which shone in the moonlight like the clouds above her, and tightened her coat against the cold. Her hand dropped to the frozen railing as she stopped at the edge of the deck, taking in the scenery.

The shoreline of the lake sat below her at the base of a gentle slope about a hundred or so feet from the stairs to her deck. The house was her little slice of paradise in the Rocky Mountains of British Columbia, Canada. In the summer months, her home was open to travellers the world over who would come and stay in her resort cabins. Miles of hiking trails ran around the lake and into the mountains nearby, promising adventure for all outdoor activities one might be interested in. Rarely, the resort would get visitors in the winter months. Most tourism in the Canadian winters was limited to ski resorts and the like, not a lakeside lodge. Today, all her cabins were empty, and Annabelle found herself alone in the frigid paradise.

A soft meow and a thudding sound caught Annabelle's attention, and she turned to see her cat trotting toward her. He was a large tomcat that had appeared at the lodge a few years back. No one knew how he had arrived there, being as remote as they were. Perhaps he had stowed away in a visitor's vehicle, but none of the guests had recognized him upon his arrival. He was well fed and acclimated to humans, with not an ounce of feral in him, so Annabelle had relented in her search for his owners and decided to adopt him. He was a great companion in the mountains, keeping the mice population down, and serving as the lovable mascot of the resort. They had named him Tank, and his hefty girth fit the bill.

"Hello, Tank," Annabelle said, bending down to pet him as he rubbed against her legs. "Nice night for hunting?"

Tank meowed and sauntered toward the door into the lodge, making his desire known by rubbing against the frame. Annabelle smiled as she crossed the deck.

"Dinner time?"

Annabelle opened the door and Tank disappeared inside. Before entering the lodge after him, Annabelle turned to take one last look at the lake. She paused. Something out in the middle of the ice had caught her attention. She closed the door and pulled her jacket tighter again as she returned to her spot against the railing. Squinting, she tried to focus on what she was seeing. Something was moving out on the ice, making its way towards the lodge. Her first thought was an animal of some sort. Most likely a Moose, or maybe a deer. It was incredibly common to see wildlife this far up in the woods. Yet it was still too far away to be sure.

Initially, Annabelle wanted to retreat to the safety of the lodge and watch whatever it was approaching from behind glass. Something about the movement though seemed strangely familiar, and so her curiosity overcame her fear. Without even realizing it, Annabelle stepped down off the porch and began making her way to the shore of the lake. Even if the shape was an animal, it was still far enough away that she could reach the lodge if she had to. But Annabelle felt no sense of danger, and as she reached the frozen shore of the lake, she realized why. The shape was human.

Still quite a way out on the ice, the figure became unmistakable in the moonlight. It was a young woman, maybe a teen or early twenties, trudging one foot in front of the other toward the lodge. Her movements were steady but erratic like she was moving in survival mode. Annabelle gasped and made her way onto the ice.

A thousand thoughts went through her mind as Annabelle rushed to the lady. How did she get here? Why is she alone? Something had happened; perhaps a snowmobiling trip met with disaster and this lady was the only one able to go for help. Somewhere deep in her mind, Annabelle felt fear as well. Alone in a mountain lodge under a moonlit sky in the Canadian winter was no place to have lone guests arriving by way of the ice.

Annabelle had been running this lodge for many years, first with her husband before his passing, and then all by herself with Tank for company. She had two sons, both with families of their own, who sometimes came to help her in the summer months. One of those sons was due to check on her in a day or so. If the situation took a turn for the worse, Annabelle knew someone would come looking for her.

At last, the distance between them closed to a range where they could see one another. The young lady collapsed to her knees on the ice, sending a rolling cracking sound through the lake. Annabelle got a good look at her then. She was young and beautiful, with striking features and long blond hair flowing from below a thick red toque. She was wearing mountain gear; black snow pants, a heavy gray coat, and white winter boots. Her breath was ragged and ejected long bursts of steam into the moonlight as she fought to catch it.

"Oh my Lord," Annabelle gasped as she slid to a stop and bent down over the young lady. "What in heavens are you doing out here? Come. Let's get you off the ice."

Wordless and still gasping for breath, the young lady shook her head. She turned and pointed back the way she had come, out across the lake to the far shore.

"There are others?" Annabelle asked.

The lady nodded.

"Well, there's not much I can do for them alone," Annabelle pleaded. "Let's get you off the ice and we'll call in search and rescue."

The lady frantically waved her arms. Their eyes met and in the young ladies, Annabelle saw a desperate pleading fear. She realized the lady's coat was torn. Animal attack? She looked as though she was on the verge of passing out. Annabelle's mind raced.

"Look" she began, dropping to her knees to be eye-to-eye with the lady. "Tell me what happened. I'll get you off the ice and get search and rescue out to look for the others. How many are you? What were you doing out here?"

The young lady shook. She pointed again, gasping for breath. Her tears ran down her cheeks like diamond droplets in the moonlight.

"I don't understand…"

Annabelle's voice trailed off. In frustration, she had followed the young lady's insistent beckoning, only this time she saw another shape far out in the center of the lake. This one was not moving, a dark lump barely visible against the black ice reflecting the starlit sky above. Annabelle understood immediately.

"Try to get to the lodge," she said as she stood. "There's food and warmth. I'll be there as soon as I can!"

With that, Annabelle was off across the ice. Mentally, she began a checklist for first aid and thought of all the potential injuries she might encounter. The young lady's clothing was torn. If it was an animal attack, there could be excessive blood loss. Broken bones. Almost a certainty there would be hypothermia and shock. Annabelle steeled herself for the worst as she made her way further out onto the lake. The ice was thick beneath her feet. More than once she considered going back for a snowmobile. There was enough freeze to handle the weight. No time, she thought to herself, and she pressed on.

Farther and farther, she went out onto the dark ice. She kept her eyes on the shape she was approaching, adrenaline steeling her to the cold and forcing her legs to keep moving. She thought of her sons, and what they might have done had they been here. Surely they would have gone out into the dark while she stayed in the warmth of the lodge, waiting to tend to whoever they recovered. She was always the nurturing type, caring for everyone lost or otherwise. Tank was a prime example. At the thought of Tank, Annabelle stole a glance back over her shoulder.

The young lady was nowhere to be seen. Had she made it to the lodge already? Found a second wind? Cold fear froze Annabelle in place like she had become a part of the lake ice itself. The moonlit sky and its haunting white clouds suddenly felt oppressive where only moments before it was peaceful and serene. The frozen lake, its dark mass webbed by cracks and frozen bubbles shining against the blackness was now ominous and foreboding.

Annabelle squinted and searched the darkness. The snow that still coated the trees and the shore was glowing in the moonlight. The warm yellow light of the lodge shone out, a solitary spike of colour against the gray-scale contrast of the winter scenery. Nothing moved. It was like the woman had never been there in the first place. She swung her head wild, searching for anything other than herself in the abyssal expanse of ice. Nothing. Not even the shape she had been making her way toward was there anymore. It was like the lake itself had tricked her.

"What the…"

Annabelle's words trailed off into the silence. She could not even bring herself to finish the sentence.

How absurd of her. The loneliness must be playing tricks on her mind, she thought. The other person was out here, and the young lady must have simply made it to the lodge. She was probably all bundled up in blankets already, soaking in heat from the hearth while Tank purred and rubbed against her. People never just appeared and vanished up here. Annabelle did not believe in that sort of thing. Mountain lakes were not the homes of ghosts.

Annabelle scoffed at herself as she turned away from the lodge and took another step across the lake. And then she plunged. It was almost as though there had never been ice below her feet at all. She fell impossibly fast into the darkness beneath the ice. Cold water assaulted her, and the pressure built so quickly that she felt her eardrums burst. High above her, the surface swallowed what remained of the shimmering moon, and in the pitch black, shock and the pain in her ears made her scream. Before she passed out, she watched the bubbles ejected from her final breath reflect tiny silver slivers of light as they climbed to the surface. Down into the endless black she fell. Into the home of ghosts.

********

The first detail that hit me when I rolled to a stop in front of the Black Lake Lodge was the breathtaking mountains. The pictures I saw online didn't do them justice. Sharp rising peaks rimmed the

42

horizon, like the maw of some ancient worm coming up from the core of the Earth. The second detail was the lake itself. The internet said that for all but three months of every year, the water was frozen over with a thick black layer of ice. Fed by glaciers and so high in the mountains, it was a hidden gem within the Canadian Rockies. It was early October, and winter was close at hand, so the lake as it lay before me was absolutely earning its name.

Jet black ice, even in the daylight, stretched from shore to shore. A constant breeze was blowing, ensuring no snow would stick to the ice. The only detail preventing the lake from looking like a hole in time and space was a spiderweb of natural cracks and frozen bubbles on its surface. The lodge and its cabins were a silent sentinel, watching the area until time and decay ended their vigil.

I shut off the engine and opened my door. Kimi Alexander opened the passenger door and stepped out. Her long raven-black hair fell straight at her back and shimmered in the afternoon sun. I watched her step around the door as she closed it and stretched. It had been a long car ride for both of us, but Kimi was still young and not without her indigenous sense of humour.

"Wow, Nick." She began as she cracked her back. "You bring me to the nicest places."

I had met Kimi a few months after my second novel was published, while I was on tour promoting the book in Ontario. She was studying a  publishing major back then, hoping to become an editor for one of the big publishing houses. Instead, we had struck up a conversation that became the birth of our many zany adventures together. Kimi was Algonquin First Nations, one of the many indigenous peoples of Canada. She had a natural curiosity and an insatiable lust for lore and superstition. Naturally, with the subject matter of my books being what they were, she had become a fan. Eventually, we became great friends as well, and soon we were travelling the country exploring places with haunting stories tied to them.

I smiled at her and then turned to regard what she had meant. The Black Lake Lodge had a history of supernatural folklore. Abandoned a little over nine years ago when the patron mysteriously disappeared, her surviving sons had sold the property off. Not surprisingly, given its market value, the lodge and rights to the lake had turned over for a significant amount to an American looking to invest in Canada's tourism sector. A year after the sale, the new owner and his entire family of four disappeared in what the news called a 'tragic mountaineering accident.'

There had been an Unsolved Mysteries episode about the lodge, and the legend of the resort grew. It had been abandoned for quite a long time, and once again the Black Lake Lodge was up for sale. When Kimi told me about the lake and its history, it was not very hard to convince the title holders to grant us free access. I had a reputation in Canada for debunking claims of the supernatural. I think they must have thought I could bury the stigma of the place, and they would have an easier time selling it. Unfortunately, over the years of limited use and neglect, the resort had fallen into disrepair.

"Yeah I really do," I said as I closed my door and followed suit with the stretching. It certainly did feel good after being in the car for so long. "But let's not forget this trip was your bucket list, lady."

Kimi scoffed and flipped me the middle finger.

"You know I ain't no lady."

I laughed and started making my way to the main lodge building.

"Got that right."

Kimi bent down and scooped up a snowball.

"Fuck around and find out!"

Bap.

The snowball connected square between my shoulders and I laughed as I hustled forward a few steps.

"What are you thinking with this one, Nick?"

Kimi had asked me that question about fifty times now since we left Ontario. We had discussed everything in our repertoire already. Yeti. Sasquatch. Ghosts. Wild animals. Serial killers living in the woods. Kimi was a veritable encyclopedia of folklore and the supernatural. She had a gift for it, she said. Blessed by her ancestors. Even her name meant 'secret' in her language. She said it was because no one could ever keep one from her. The next words out of her mouth proved that well enough.

"You don't think we're going to find a grisly murder scene, do you, Nick? Another Breaking sorta thing?"

I stopped and drew a deep breath. My mind ached for a moment as painful memories flooded in. I was a detective before I became an author. Royal Canadian Mounted Police. It was just another weekend of bad news, mostly gang activity and the occasional drug-induced debauchery. But then a call came in I would never forget. Thomas Barrow, a regular white-collar Canadian, had gone mad and slaughtered his whole family with a kitchen knife. Only his son had remained alive and untouched. I had been the lead detective on the case, but what happened after I responded to that fateful call made me believe in things most people would not, even if they wanted to.

Nothing in my life had been the same after that case. I could not keep my career on the rails. They called it Post Traumatic Stress Disorder. Blamed the death of my daughter a year before the case. They said that the murders 'hit too close to home.' Pushed me over the edge. They had no idea because I could never tell the truth. I spent over a year at the bottom of a bottle after they took my badge until I met my therapist Josephine Walsh. She was the one who suggested I write as a cathartic exercise. Tell my story, even if it was fiction to the rest of the world.

So that is exactly what I did. I started writing about all the strange things I was seeing. Wrote about the case through the eyes of a fictional detective. Faced my truth through story, as Josephine put it. And be damned if that book didn't become a best-seller almost overnight. I used the money I made to travel. Sought out other people who had similar experiences. I began weaving their stories into my own until I had a tapestry that spanned two novels and sixteen short stories. Then I met Kimi.

One night after we had become friends, Kimi and I were sitting on the sands of Wasaga Beach, a small town on the Southern shores of Georgian Bay in Ontario. We had just finished an investigation which we had found to be a prank by a group of local teens. The papers that day were running stories about the anniversary of the Thomas Barrow murders. I was a bit too far into the whiskey, and I ended up telling Kimi what actually happened to me. I told her about a little boy who spoke of a ghost named Chadwick. A little boy who put his Father through something called the Breaking. I told her how in a way I will never be able to explain, the ghost of my daughter rewound time and prevented me from enduring the Breaking as well.

God as my witness, telling it out loud made the story sound so much more insane than my writing did. Kimi devoured every word though. This was only the second time she had brought it up in all our adventures though. She knew it was a deep wound for me, but in my heart of hearts, I believed she just wanted to remind me that it happened. She wanted me to face it, not forget it. Of all the investigating we did together, the one thing that would give me closure was the one thing I refused to investigate.

"Kimi…" I began as I stopped.

She danced past me, throwing her arms up in frustration.

"I know, I know… you don't want to talk about. I'm sorry… okay? Let's go explore the spooky cabin in the woods with the black hole lake…"

I watched her for a moment as she turned her back and kept walking toward the lodge. Then I bent down.

Bap.

The snowball connected bullseye in the back of her head. She froze and spun toward me like a marionette doll sporting a cheeky smile.

"Fuck around and find out" I mocked her.

"You… mother…" words caught in her throat and her eyes went wide in shock. For a second my heart stopped at the true fear in her eyes until I followed her gaze down to her feet.

A huge gray-striped tabby had appeared and was rubbing himself on Kimi's legs. He meowed as he carved a figure-eight pattern into the snow while purring against her boots. Shock turned to adoration as Kimi bent down and scooped the friendly feline up into her arms. I could see this was a chore for her. It was quite a meaty cat.

"You scared the SHIT out of me, cat!" Kimi said as she held him up to look into his eyes. She noticed the collar on him and brought him in to snuggle against her chest, which he clearly enjoyed. I approached as she scratched his neck and then lifted the tag on his collar.

"Holy shit!" She squeaked as she erupted in laughter. "This chonky bugger's name is TANK!"

Her laughter was infectious as I reached out to see for myself.

"Really?" I said through fits of laughter. I lifted the tag to see for myself. The writing on the little metal disc said 'My name is Tank. If found, please notify the Black Lake Lodge. 555-323-7743.'

"Well, how about that? Old boy too, by the looks of things. Must be a great hunter to keep that much weight up here alone."

Kimi lowered Tank to the ground but he remained near her.

"I wonder how old he is? Sure looks like his youth is behind him."

I shrugged.

"Hard to say. I've read a lot about this place, and the website mentions a mascot but doesn't mention specifics. Maybe it's him. That would put him up there in years for sure if he belonged to Annabelle Lewis."

Kimi turned and started her walk toward the lodge again. She beckoned for Tank to follow and he bounced after her, using her footprints as a path through the snow. I turned back to the car.

"I'll get our stuff and meet you inside."

Kimi waved without looking back at me.
"Sure thing boss!"

*******

The Lodge was a beautiful structure, even as run down as it was. A large deck overlooked a gentle slope down to the lake shore, and the whole front of the building was mostly glass. The panes showed years of wear without cleaning and now were fogged in places and chipped by wind-blown debris. A few cracks skirted the corners, but nothing that threatened the integrity of the panes. The building was a log-cabin type construction with a high a-frame peaked roof. The interior was mostly open-concept space with a huge stone hearth on the left-hand wall as you entered from the deck. A cluster of three high-back lounge chairs and a round oak table sat in front of the fireplace in the hearth, one of which was now claimed by a content-looking Tank. Right away we saw how Tank had been maintaining his supple size. A pet door had been installed and an auto-feeder kept his dish constantly filled.

To the right of the main door was a meagre kitchen built along the wall. It was part of the main room, separated only by a stunning live-edge island surrounded by stools. In the back of the open main space, a short hallway disappeared under an open landing, leading to storage, laundry, and the main bathroom. Stairs leading to the second-floor landing were set against the left wall past the hearth, and two bedrooms capped off the floor plan. The master bedroom was one of the rooms upstairs, and it was equipped with an elegant en-suite bathroom. Not surprisingly, Kimi called shotgun on the master bedroom.

I had been assured by the current title holders that the power was still on at the Lodge and that all the amenities were functioning. Kimi and I were elated to discover this was indeed the case. We took turns having a hot shower and then cooked a decent meal for ourselves using the supplies we had brought with us. The entire time we made small talk about the trip, our work, and the history of the Lodge itself.

Kimi had done what she could through her usual channels. She had found the property was first built by Irish settlers during the Western expansion of Canada before the railroad even made its way through the Rockies. Some paraphernalia from those homesteading days decorated the lodge, like old wood-woven snowshoes, and an antique jar with a letter claiming it had carried water from an Irish lock that was added to the lake for a little piece of home. Going back even further in the lake's history, she found anecdotes that the local indigenous peoples had frequently used Black Lake as a camp during their mountain hunts to shelter from the harsh high-elevation weather. The history of the lake fascinated Kimi, and in turn, her passion rubbed off on me. I listened to her with rapt attention.

Yet in all the lore on this place, nothing until the disappearance of Annabelle Lewis stood out as a potential lead. There was no history of curses, murderers, cryptids, or anything out of the ordinary. It seemed a place of idyllic tranquillity, and I tried hard to fathom the horrors that had happened here. There was nothing in this place but absolute calm, especially once Kimi and I were sitting on the deck enjoying a hot rum under the moonlight.

"Look at how the moonlight makes the cracks in the ice glow…" Kimi said as she gestured with her cup at the lake. Tank was curled up and purring in her lap. "Looks like space itself is a mirror that broke."

I smiled at her description. The moonlight indeed made the snow-capped peaks, the trees, and the white cracks and frozen bubbles seem to glow against the bleak darkness of the deep lake. The sky was nearly cloudless, and the stars were more numerous in the sky than anywhere I had ever been. Ontario had too many cities, densely packed, to find this lack of light pollution. In all but the most remote places, Canada's central Provinces just could not compare. This place, an infinitely serene location in the high mountains, felt like the middle of the Pacific Ocean. Other than Kimi and Tank, I felt further from humanity than I ever had before. It was relaxing, all the way to my soul.

A ringing sound startled me out of my trance. Kimi looked at me, her face a mix of disgust and surprise.

"Are you kidding me? How the HELL do you have cell service here?"

I laughed as I fished my phone out of my pocket.

"I don't Kimi. It's the lodges satellite internet."

I stood and started making my way to the door.

"Still doesn't explain why your phone works, Nick…"

I stopped and turned back, smiling. It was rare at my age that I was able to gloat about my knowledge of technology.

"WiFi calling, Kimi. Get a good phone."

Kimi laughed as I turned back toward the door.

"You're lucky Tank is comfortable or I'd throw something at you."

I taunted her as I stepped through the door into the house.

"All you have near you to throw is your drink, and I know you won't waste that!"

I didn't give Kimi a chance to respond before the door was closed. I answered the phone.

"Hello?"

"Nick, hi. It's Josephine. I wanted to check in, and see how you're doing and how the trip went."

"Hey, Josephine. Thanks for the call. The trip went well. Kimi and I are at the Black Lake Lodge now. Got here this afternoon."

"Good. I'm glad to hear it. I know we didn't have an appointment scheduled, I just wanted to check in because…"

"Because tomorrow is the anniversary" I

interrupted. I knew exactly what she meant.

"Yes."

"You know…" I began after a short silence. "Kimi brought it up today. She's been speculating what we might find here since we left Ontario. Just as we arrived, she asked if I thought we'd find a grisly murder scene."

"How did that make you feel?"

"Alright. I guess. I don't know for sure, to be honest. The dreams haven't happened in a long time, and there's never been any visits from…" This time it was my voice that trailed off. Her name caught in my throat.

"Sandra?" Josephine asked.

"Yeah."

"When are you coming back, Nick? I'd like to pick up our sessions again. I feel like maybe you need someone to talk to."

"I have Kimi."

"True, and I'm thankful for that, Nick. But I think it's been too long since our last sessions. I'm just looking out for you Nick. That's all."

"I know, Josephine. We likely won't be here longer than a couple of days. It's quiet here. Serene. Do you have time maybe next week?"

"Let me check my calendar. One second here."

While I waited for Josephine to continue, I paced the room. An old fire poker resting against the stone hearth caught my attention and I approached it. I picked it up in my hands and turned it over, examining the hard steel rod. It was heavy. Maybe iron. Old, it was spotted with rust and the handle made of carved wood was graying and cracked. It looked like at one time it may have been a ski pole or a hiking rod. Soot stains near its tip made it clear the new purpose it served was as a fire poker.

"I can do next Thursday the 25th of August at 3 PM if that works for you, Nick? Gives you ten days to get home."

I lowered the fire poker back to its resting place against the hearth and turned back to the window. Kimi was standing against the railing staring out at the lake.

"Sounds good Josephine."

Suddenly Kimi turned and was bolting toward the door to the lodge.

"I'm glad to hear your voice, Nick, and I'm happy to hear you in high spirits considering the…"

Josephine's words were cut off by Kimi yanking the door open. She was excited and breathless.

"There's someone out on the ice, Nick! They look hurt."

I started moving toward the door.

"Sorry Josephine, I have to go. I'll call you back when I can."

I barely heard Jospehine's reply before the phone was hung up and dropped into my pocket. Together, Kimi and I crossed the deck and stopped against the railing. My eyes searched the dark lake with fervour, not knowing what I might see. Empty black ice stared back.

"Where?" I asked tentatively, my heavy breath fogging in the cold night air.

"Whoa. There was someone there, Nick. I swear it. Just a moment or two ago… out that way in the middle of the ice."

Kimi pointed almost straight out from the lodge, across the lake where a sharp peak rose against the moon and star-lit sky.

"Looked like a young woman, wearing snow clothes. Holding her arms. Maybe hurt? I don't know… she was far out, and looked like she was limping."

I squinted at the dark water, trying with all my might to pierce the darkness. My mind raced through investigative procedures that helped me in the past, and I searched for details over the last few days to discern the possibility of other people being out here. I remembered the title owner saying no other people would be staying at the lodge or in the cabins, but he did mention the possibility of hunters or snowmobile groups in the area this time of year. The waitress at the diner we ate at before making our way up to the lodge asked if we were hunting too. Could be an animal attack, or an accident. Could be something more.

"There!" Kimi shouted and pointed just off the direction she originally had. "There! A dark spot on the ice. She must have collapsed! Let's go!"

Kimi was off like a rocket.

"Kimi wait!" I shouted. "We don't know how thick the ice is!"

Kimi ignored me. She was almost halfway down the slope to the shore.

"Fuck…"

As I started after her I stopped. A tingle at the back of my neck made me rush back into the house. I scooped up the ski-pole fire poker, and then I was rushing after my friend, barreling out into the frozen darkness beyond.

********

The ice was not as slick as I expected it to be, and though at times my footing did slide a little bit, for the most part, my boots gripped the surface and I was able to make decent time catching up to Kimi. Fortunately for me, after about thirty meters onto the ice, she had slowed considerably and I was able to catch up. She was still moving toward the shape out in the middle of the lake but at a more measured pace. She almost seemed relieved when I caught up.

"My knight in shining armor" she joked as we pushed on into the darkness.

"What?" I said, straining to keep my eyes on the dark form out on the ice.

"You brought a sword."

I realized Kimi was referring not only to the fire poker I brought with me but the way I was gripping it by the handle. It looked like a sword. I dared to giggle a little bit at how ridiculous I must look. Moonlit and charging across a black frozen lake in the remote mountains, wielding an old metal fire poker like it were Excalibur.

"Shut up."

"Can you see her? Fuck it's hard to see in the dark. Should have brought a flashlight."

Kimi's words gave me pause for a second, and I reached into my pocket. I pulled out my phone and pressed the torch button. Immediately the black ice at our feet changed to a more bluish tone. I passed the phone to Kimi and she shone it forward. The light caught a pile of colour not far off in the distance. Blonde hair. A red toque. Gray coat.

The figure had collapsed on the ice with its back facing us, almost in a fetal position. From the position of the body, I guessed perhaps hypothermia or exhaustion had caused the collapse, but the hair on the back of my neck was standing up regardless. I slowed my pace, and sensing my trepidation, so did Kimi. We approached steadily, but cautiously. A lone figure appearing at the center of a dark lake with so much recent mystery raised our suspicions.

I could not help myself as we crept ever closer. I thought of Thomas Barrow. I saw him in the interrogation chair, saw the creepy gray-brown vomit sliding from his mouth as blackish blood oozed from his ears and tear ducts. I had spent years after that experience hunting the paranormal and the supernatural, and my instincts were screaming at me now, no matter how much my eyes told me this woman needed help. There was just something else at the edge of my senses, and I gripped the ski pole tighter in my hands.

"Hello?" Kimi called out. Her sudden speech startled me a bit. "Sorry, Nick…" she whispered to me.

"It's okay" I whispered back, barely aware of my response.

"Are you hurt? We're here to help you" Kimi continued.

We were maybe six or so meters away from the figure now, and we could see it was breathing. The coat was shuddering, and there was a prominent rise and fall of the chest. The closer we approached, the more details I was able to gather. The person's frame was small, wearing black snow pants under a gray coat and what looked to be white snow boots. Cognizant of misgendering the individual, my intuition was leaning toward a young woman. My thoughts were confirmed when the figure weekly rose to her knees and turned to us.

She was maybe early twenties. Fine of feature, with a sharp jawline and a narrow nose. European descent likely, especially when the phone torch illuminated her bright green eyes. Straight blonde hair fell past her shoulders, partly hidden below that bright red toque she wore. She had been crying, evident by the stains on her cheeks from running eyeliner. Her gloved hands clutched her chest at the end of crossed arms, a common indication of cold. I stopped a meter or so away, and Kimi slowly dropped to her knees a bit closer.

"Are you okay?" Kimi asked.

The girl looked terrified. She opened her mouth as if to speak, but instead, she turned and pointed further out onto the ice. Kimi followed her pointing with the flashlight.

"I don't understand…" Kimi said, searching the darkness in the direction the young woman was pointing with the light. The torch on the phone was ineffective beyond only a short distance, and neither of us could see what she was referring to. Was there someone else? Was an animal chasing her? All the possibilities pin-balled within my mind. Kimi relented the search first, deciding that this young woman warranted our current focus, and she turned the light back on her as she reached out.

The young woman spun shockingly fast and recoiled from Kimi's near touch.

"It's okay…" I said, stepping forward and holding my hand out. "We won't hurt you. We just want to help."

The young woman turned her attention to me and froze in place when she saw the metal fire poker in my hand. Her breathing quickened, her fingers digging into her coat, her muscles coiling as if to run in fright.

Immediately I held out my hands to show I was not a threat.

"It's okay…" I began. "I won't hurt you. Look… I'll put this down."

The young woman watched me like a hawk as I slowly lowered the poker toward the ice. She seemed to become more afraid the closer the metal got to the surface of the lake. A whisper rose inside my skull like a ringing bell.

"Dad…"

I stopped dead in my motion. My heart froze like the ice on the lake.

"Sandra?" I whispered.

Kimi spun on me but kept the light on the young woman.

"What the fuck did you say?" Kimi hissed.

My eyes were locked. I wasn't seeing Kimi or the girl. I was searching my mind for that whisper.

"Dad," it came again, clearer now. Closer. "Dad look without your eyes."

I blinked, confused.

"What?"

"Look without your eyes, Dad."

"I don't understand… Sandra… what do you mean? How do I look without my eyes?"

"You're scaring the shit out of me here, Nick," Kimi said.

Then it hit me. I focused my eyesight in the darkness beyond the young woman but kept her in my peripheral vision. I kept staring until the focus made my vision blur and my eyes water.

"Nick, what the fu…"

And then the young woman was gone. Further out on the ice, something charged towards us, like a shadow in the ice itself. It had no form, nothing I could focus on anyway. Just a shadow, galloping toward us impossibly fast. Before I had a chance to warn her, it lunged and Kimi fell through the ice.

"No!" I screamed, and dove forward as fast as the slippery traction would allow. I was just fast enough. I fell prone on the ice, and my free arm shot into the dark water of the hole where Kimi had been. I grasped her under her armpits, and she wrapped her arms around my neck in panic. Her face was bobbing just above the surface of the water. My lungs burned from my yell.

"Nick…" she gasped, desperate to keep her face above the water. "Fuck Nick something is pulling me down!"

"I've got you!" I called back, even as I felt myself sliding into the hole, and heard the ice cracking beneath my chest.

"Don't let go, Nick!" Kimi screamed, water bubbling in her mouth as her face dipped below the surface.

"Use the iron…" the whisper exploded in my mind.

Understanding immediately, I twisted enough to lift the fire poker into the air, and then slammed it down, spiking the sharp tip into the ice. I was only hoping for an anchor to use as leverage to get Kimi out of the hole, but when the tip of that poker touched the ice it was like the entire lake bellowed.

There was no real sound in the force that rolled over us in reaction to the poker stabbing into the ice. Not in the sense of a normal sound, but more like a reverberation that echoed inside our minds and seemed to roll across the lake, through the trees, and into the mountain itself. Pain. It caused the lake pain. I did not hesitate to seize the opening, and with every ounce of my strength, I yanked Kimi free of the hole.

Kimi collapsed on the ice beside me, shivering uncontrollably. I rolled over and put my hands on her, dragging her further from the hole onto solid ice. The fire poker, embedded upright in the ice like a flag pole, was near my feet now. Kimi was conscious, struggling to breathe, and clearly in shock.

"Kimi… Kimi are you okay?"

"S… so cold…" she squeaked between shivers.

"I'll get you inside… I'll…"

A shiver ran down my spine, and I turned to see a shape of darkness and frigid water rising from the broken hole in the ice. At first, the shape was bulbous and malformed, like water gushing up from a broken line underground, but as it rose higher from the hole, appendages sprouted from it and a head took shape. It looked like a horse. A nightmare steed from the frozen depths of hell, slowly climbing from the lake. I could feel fury radiating from it. As I finally regained control of my shocked muscle, I tried to kick away and my foot tapped the fire poker. Instantly the horse recoiled, and for a moment it lost its form.

"Strike now Dad!" Sandra's voice was a scream inside my skull that made my eyes blur with tears. Again I acted swiftly.

I summoned every ounce of strength inside me and lunged for the poker. In a fluid motion, I pulled the metal pole from the ice and swung with all my might in an upward arc. The poker swished through the shadowy water of the horse right about where I thought its neck would be. There was a gurgling sound as a huge swath of water detached from the main body surging from the hole. It splashed all over me and the ice I stood on. The cold I felt from the water was like needles in my skin.

The demon horse melted back into the lake, and somehow the ice at my feet became brighter, taking on more of the common colour one would expect from a frozen lake. I was shaking, both from the cold and the adrenaline surging through my veins. My breath was deep and gasping. Other than the shared shivering between Kimi and me, the lake was silent and serene again. I coughed and doubled over. The adrenaline was wearing off and the cold was setting in. My breath was like a cloud ejecting from my face.

"Sandra…" I whispered. There was no answer. "Sandra?" Silence. Only our ragged breathing.

I looked down at the hole where Kimi had gone through the ice. The hole the horse monster had come from, and I drew a sharp breath. I wanted to cry. My body shook violently, and I could feel my muscles stiffening. Was I losing my damn mind? That could not have been real. I sank to my knees on the ice. It was getting harder to breathe, and the line between shock and panic was blurring. My attention turned for a moment to the metal pole. My hands shaking, I held it out and dropped it point first into the darkness below the ice.

Fearing my ability to get back to safety if I lingered any longer, I grabbed hold of Kimi's jacket and started dragging her toward the lodge. She gave me purpose, despite my wanting to curl up and die. I felt so lost in the darkness, so I narrowed my scope. I ignored the sweeping vista surrounding me and locked my eyes on the speck of bright colour the lodge provided. I let it become the candle that lit my way as I soldiered on across the lake.

********

I don't know how long it took to drag Kimi across the ice and up the slope to the lodge, but I remember intimately how it felt when that door swung open and I felt heat kiss my face. Tank watched with concern as I shuffled across the floor dragging a now unconscious Kimi with me. I laid her on the floor before the burning fire in the hearth, and then stripped my wet clothes, tossing them into a pile near one of the chairs. I scooped warm blankets from the seating areas, including the one Tank had been sleeping on. He did not seem to mind, instead sitting on the floor and beginning to lick his paws.

Kimi was shivering slightly, and her breathing was shallow. Her lips had turned blue. Recalling my first aid training, I knew shivering was a good sign. She had not progressed too far into her hypothermia yet. I stripped her clothes too, down to her underwear, before covering us both with the dry blankets and holding her close near the fire. I held her tight in my arms, not a thought given to the intimate contact but purely to the survival of both of us. Eventually, her shivering stopped, and I started to drift off to sleep.

"Dad…" Sandra whispered.

I squinted my eyes tight.

"Dad…"

"Sandra?"

"Hi, Dad."

"Am I dreaming?"

"Not yet… you're in the place between asleep and awake. I needed to speak to you."

"Sandra, what is happening? Am I going crazy?"

"No Dad… listen… I don't have much time."

"Sandra this is crazy. What was that in the lake?"

"An old monster Dad, it's gone now."

"Wait… Nathan Barrow mentioned the place between asleep and awake. He said…"

"He said that's where he spoke to Chadwick."

"Yes."

"Dad listen… Chadwick is not what you think it is. It's not a person. It's something else… something dangerous. Chadwick has broken things… things in the veil."

"How do you know that?"

"Because I'm in the same place he is. Dad… Listen. Please."

"Okay."

"You need to stay with Kimi. You need to hunt the Breaking together."

"Sandra… you told me not to…"

"Dad!" her voice hurt inside my brain.

"Dad… you need to stop the Breaking."

"Why me?"

"Because you're the only one who can. Because you're connected to me."

"What do you…"

"I'm part of it, Dad."

"What do you mean?"

Silence.

"Sandra?"

Silence.

"Sandra!"

"Hunt… the Breaking… Dad."

The darkness of sleep crept over me then, and Sandra's voice faded into a dream.

********

When I woke, the sun was peering over the mountain peaks bathing the lake and the outside world in a light orange glow. Kimi was still wrapped in my arms under the blankets, and her breathing was slow and relaxed. I thought about the words Sandra had said. Nothing made sense, but a determination was lit within me, and I knew what I had to do. I lifted my head and looked at Kimi's raven hair. Her eyes were open and she was looking at the sunrise.

"How are you feeling?" I asked.

"Like we're shacked up" she replied with a coy smile.

"Kimi… nothing happened. I was trying to get you warm."

Kimi laughed and rolled over to look at me.

"You think I don't know that? Come on, Nick. I'm messing with you."

Her tone suddenly shifted, and her eyes fell out of focus like she was seeing something far beyond me.

"Nick…" she began, swallowing as if the words hurt her throat. "Did a demon water horse try to eat me last night?"

"Yeah… something like that…"

Kimi nodded, processing.

"And you chopped its head off with a fire poker, right?"

"Yeah."

"We're not crazy… right?"

I paused for a long moment before answering her. "No."

"Okay, just checking."

Kimi nestled into my chest.

"Glad you brought that sword."

I lowered my chin to rest on the top of her head. "Me too."

We lay for a time like that in silence, Tank cuddled up on the blankets at Kimi's feet.

"Water horse fucked around…" Kimi said quietly.

"And it found out." I finished.

Outside, dawn crept over the mountains and illuminated a bluish-white lake, with a run-down lodge and cabins settled within peaks that spiked high into the Canadian sky.

"Kimi…"

"Mmm-hmm?"

"I'm going to hunt the Breaking."

There was a long pause, and I wondered if maybe Kimi had lost her interest after the night's events. Kimi shuffled against me, pulling the blankets tighter around herself.

"Sounds good, Nick. Give me five more minutes."


LA FIN

… or is it?

# NECROMANTIC

I was a Bard once. A troubadour travelling the land and spinning tales through music to delight and educate. From tavern to tavern, town square to town square, I wandered and sang and danced and played. There were always those who stayed behind after my performances, hoping to garner some of my wisdom and hear more stories of my travel. I delighted in my life of fame and moderate fortune. I was sought after by kings.

Alas, all the joy and heartache I had experienced could not prepare me for the day I met *her*. Hear now my tale, faithful patron. Listen, as I regale you with a story of love beyond life, and the bitter betrayal to come.

The room was cold, yet flooded with the warm glow of candles. Many candles, perhaps more than should have been, burned back the darkness. A fog obscured my vision at first, like the mist on a river at dawn, it relented to the candlelight as though it were the rising sun. As the world became ever more visible, stone walls, gothic decorations, and dark wooden bookshelves boxed me in. But the burgeoning clarity of my sight ceased, as though while waking, the sleepy blur of sticky eyes remained. Try as I might, I could not wash it away. In my hazy sight, a dark form rose before me. A realization came to me. The form was my own.

The strangest of sensations came over me. Terror burned like torch fire through my soul, as I watched my fetid corpse rise to a seated position upon a stone slab before me. A detached sense of disbelief, tempered by curiosity yet still alight with the heat of anger and fear, captured my attention. Through a milky lens, I watched my body rise from the table, clothing in tatters, hair matted with grime. Once upright, the grisly shadow of my former self sank to its knees in supplication. It was only then I noticed the figure that stood at the foot of the stone table, arms outstretched, fingers splayed. My heart did not pound as it should have. I lifted my hands before my face and beheld. I was a mere spirit.

Had I been able, I would have sundered the stone walls with my scream. My rage at this most unholy sacrilege was beyond my ability to describe. Soundless in the space between living and dead, I lashed out at the necromancer standing over my reanimated corpse.

My flailing limbs passed harmlessly through the cloaked head. With crushing sadness, I realized I was impotent. Fear gripped me. Was my spirit doomed to roam unseen in the veil as long as my body remained in service to the one who raised it? As I floated adrift, silently sobbing, the necromancer withdrew the dark hood and I beheld her for the first time.

Had I any breath within my ghostly lungs, it would have been snatched away at the sight of her. Enraptured, I drifted closer as she circled my kneeling corpse. Her movements carried an air of self-satisfaction and accomplishment, whispering of a dark magnetic power. Her smile, like a sword fit for kings, cleaved my anger. Though her form seemed to shiver through my apparition eyes, I was captivated by her features. The way her lips parted ever so slightly to tease the row of snow-white teeth behind them, the fullness and colour of her elegant lips, all ignited a longing to taste her kiss. Her shining eyes, with flecks of brown amid brilliant emerald green, drew me to her as a stone when dropped to the ground. Even the bounce of her raven-black hair as it swept over her shoulders in time with her footfall elicited the calm and serenity of a warm meadow breeze. She was glorious. Then she stopped to face my corpse once more. Her voice echoed forth and I found myself set adrift.

She began chanting in crescendos, her voice echoing in the chamber until it became a chorus of harmonizing tones. The sound was heavenly, and in mere moments I was completely ensnared. Though intangible, I found my spirit dancing to the rhythm of her song. I found rapture in the melody; a bliss that rolled through the barrier between life and death to reverberate in my soul. I found myself reliving the day I died at the tip of a bandit's spear. I felt no pain seeing my blood spill from the wound again. Instead, I felt ecstasy that my death had led me to her. To her song.

And then the chanting ended, as did my trance. I floated peacefully in the not-quite-beyond, listening eagerly for those notes. Praying I would hear that song once more, but it never came. I looked upon her, standing over my kneeling corpse, and saw she wore that angelic smile again. It grew more pronounced as my body rose to stand before her. She brushed the back of her hand against the jaw of my body. Never have I been more jealous of a simple touch. In a whisper, she said, "We shall do great things together."

I tried to speak, to pledge myself to her, but I found I had no voice in the veil. Intangible, invisible, and soundless; I was nothing more than an observer. I would never be able to share how I felt about this powerful and commanding woman. All I could do was float near her, and so I did for the weeks and months to come. As she slept I kept a silent vigil, just as my body kept stoic watch over her in the world of the living. We were a duplicate attendant to all her motions. I watched her study her dark tomes, feeling the ripples of danger that emanated from the books. I watched as she muddied herself to the elbow building a large, hideous statue from clay, vine, and swamp moss. Whatever she did, I watched, recording every minute detail.

Days blended together as I followed her on her sojourns beyond the buried crypt in the graveyard she called home. I chased away phantoms, poltergeists, wraiths, and other denizens of the afterlife that dared approach her. I wanted to warn her every time I saw a knight or a bandit sneaking through the tombstones. I yearned to protect my beloved, who had brought me life beyond the grave. Though she could not see me, my flesh took the action I could not. Repeated assaults had taken their toll on it, but the shambling corpse had always managed to keep her safe.

She revered her 'creation', as she often referred to my corpse. Yet she often inflicted abuses upon it. For a time once, my stumbling body was limping because of a gash endured to the thigh from a knight's blade. She had commanded a ceramic bowl be brought to her, and the shambling corpse dropped the bowl, shattering it on the cobblestone floor of her lair. She responded by removing both arms with a vicious dagger assault. Later that same day, she threaded the arms back on with twine and ensured they could still function. The corpse never responded, but it warmed my heart to see her caring for what once belonged to me. I yearned ever more to be with her.

The months became years, and the magic that

animated my risen body began to fade. Flesh rotted and hung from the face. Fingers were attached only by her twine-stitching and the strength of her will. Still, she cared for my body, and I loved her all the more deeply. We had come so far, her and I. Neither able to touch, or to communicate, yet still I felt we had a transcendent devotion. I learned that time was infinite in the veil, but I knew a day would come when we could be together. Life would wane for her, and eventually, her death would unite us. She had aged so little with only a few grey strands showing amid the blackness of her hair. Still, I waited.

One evening, she drifted across the stone floor while working on her beastly statue. What remained of my corpse sat across the room, lifelessly awaiting its next command. On the table where so long ago she reanimated my body, the mutilated carcass of a goat now lay. Its blood painted rivulets of crimson down to the floor. I watched her, as always, captivated by that smile. She removed and carried the goat's heart to stand before the statue. Then she reached out with both hands, bowing her head as she raised the heart and set it within a depression in the statue's chest. Once the heart was nestled in place, she returned to the table and wiped her bloody hands clean on the goat's fur before flipping the pages of one of her ancient texts.

"At last, my faithful creation," she said as she tilted her face to my corpse. "The time has come to welcome your replacement into this world."

She lifted the tome and walked to stand before her statue. Then her song began again. I was elated to finally hear her sing once more. As before, the notes rose and fell, blending until they formed a tangible force in the room. The chant rolled like the crashing of waves on a shore. I lost myself in it, succumbing to the majesty of her spell. My sight dimmed, but I paid no heed. She consumed my very soul with the sounds of her voice. At last only blackness remained, and within it, my love for her burned throughout.

The song ended abruptly. I tried to open my eyes, but found something hanging over them, blocking my vision. An odd sensation rippled through me, starting in my fingers and spreading to my whole body. My body. I could feel it. Not quite life, but not the veil which I had become accustomed to. The force of gravity was present once more, gluing my feet to the earth. The feeling of air upon my skin. The power of muscle and bone. Something rubbed across my eyes and I blinked. She was standing before me, looking directly into my eyes, having just rubbed mud away from them. My heart raced, but was it my heart? I lifted my hands before my eyes, watching as she cautiously backed away. I beheld neither flesh nor bone before me. I saw only clay, moss, and vines in the shape of hands. I heard her speak to me, directly, for the first time.

"Golem."

Confusion gripped me. Did she not know my name? After all this time had she not bothered to learn such a small detail about me? And then I looked upon her; truly saw her for the first time. The illusion that had been cast upon my spirit when she raised my corpse shimmered and fell away like a wolf shedding snow. I saw not the flawless picture of power and wonder I had believed her to be. Instead, I saw a haggard, rotting vestige, barely clinging to life. A frail old crone, with a half-bald head of wispy grey hair that looked more like the moss that hung from alpine trees stood before me. A slumped and misshapen body draped in tattered filthy rags. A sickness rose from deep within my spirit, bringing with it the anger and fear I had felt when first she raised my body.

My mind shattered into a million reflected memories, now finally clear of the spell upon my soul. I saw the innocents she forced my body to murder. I saw the tortures she inflicted on both men and animals. I saw the ghosts I had chased off for what they truly were: vengeful spirits longing to sate their desire for justice. I had been in love with a lie. Somehow beholden to the force that drove my decaying flesh into servitude.

She reached for me and said in a broken voice "Great Golem, I welcome you to the land of the living. Tell me the name of the spirit that drives you."

After many years of longing, I could not help but want the feel of her touch. When at last her fingers met my face, it was not warmth I felt, but the burning heat of rage. Beyond words, I raised a horrid clay arm and pointed at the rotting remains of my body, slumped and discarded in the corner. She followed my gesture and I saw the terror birthed within her eyes. I watched as she stumbled backward against the table, her hand bracing herself from falling as the other grasped the rags above her heart.

I was frozen, despite the new body I found myself in. It was all I could do but watch as she fought for breath. I yearned to unleash my anger upon her. To bash her horrid existence into oblivion with the incredible power of the golem. Instead, I watched her frail body fail her. I watched her once angelic lips turn blue. I watched her once powerful form quake with weakness in its passing. I thought back to her song as she died on the floor before me, hearing not the rapturous melody I yearned for, but a banshee wail of chaos and evil. When at last her struggle for breath ended, I knelt before her corpse.

Hate and pity were at war within me. The sting of love had not entirely faded to anger. I searched her still face for any glimpse of the woman I had once admired but saw none of it. The truth of betrayal had lit a fire within my soul, and I drew as deep a breath as the new body would allow. The wail that echoed forth was thunder within the lair, and the stone quivered. Dust and chips rained from the ceiling under the assault, and the candles flickered. I closed my eyes and turned away from her corpse. There was nothing more I wanted to see. I stood, and my eyes opened, and there she was.

Her spirit floated in the room, exactly as I had

always seen her. Powerful. Rapturous. Radiant. She looked lost, as though trying to come to grips with her passing. When our eyes met, I knew at once she was seeing the real me, not my risen corpse or the golem she had confined me to, but the real me. The soul that had followed her all these years.

"I…" she began, but could not find words.

Silently, I watched as her spirit wept. I felt her guilt. Her shame. I did not feel sympathy. Her spirit tried to come closer to me, but I took a step back and she hesitated. Her outstretched hand fell. I could see by the way her face lowered that she knew the pain she had caused me. The pain she had caused so many others. Then I saw a new emotion on her face as a sound echoed within the lair. Her eyes darted around the room, looking past me at something I had not yet sensed. I turned and beheld all the souls I had chased off. They had come for her. Their justice was at hand, and I wanted no part of it.

I took one last look at her before I left that lair forever. In the eyes of her spirit, I saw only pleading. Begging to be saved once more. This time, she would have no spirit to save her beyond the veil. She had no flesh to protect her as she slept. She was bare, and judgment had come for her. I do not know what became of her spirit after I left her to the ghosts of her sins. I know not if a spirit can die again, but I know now that one may feel pain. I heard it in her terrified screams fading into the darkness as I walked away.

I have since watched the ages of the Earth slip past. I have endured winters and experienced summers beyond count. I was chased from kingdom upon kingdom, hunted as the monster she had made me. I had been given the curse of life everlasting. I was immortal, indestructible, and utterly alone. Many times I wished for the release of eternal slumber. Doomed to wander beyond the touch of time, I consigned myself to exile. I found solace in the few remaining wilds of the world. Found peace in the caves of the earth. I felt there was nothing more to see in this life, and so I hid in the darkness underground. Yet now I find myself once more, completely unprepared. I see I was wrong.

As am I, you are also lost and alone. For reasons all your own, you found yourself in the woods without shelter or support. Exhausted, and afraid, you found a cave in the mountainside and chose to sleep within it. A bed of hard stone, vine, and moss seemed a perfect place for respite as you sought refuge. Then the stone spoke, and for a time, you were terrified. You considered running back into the woods, but something stayed your feet. A kindness in the voice. A kindred spirit among those who are forgotten. You chose instead to listen, without fear, and your intuition rewarded you. It rewarded both of us, for now, my faith is renewed. This day is a new dawn among the many I have seen.

For this day, I meet *you.*

# THE TASTE OF TEARS

The Esso station South of Topley Landing British Columbia was unusually busy for the time of day, even though only a single pickup truck was fueling at the pumps and a small grey-blue sedan was pulling away. The station was a quaint service center on the outskirts of town, with two fuel pumps, and a pair of tables inside with the usual amenities found in Canadian gas stations. The midday autumn sun was shining through a partly cloudy sky.

Aiyana shrugged her backpack up onto her shoulders and adjusted the scarf wound tight around her neck. She looked both ways, despite the lack of traffic, and crossed the street to the station. The driver of the pickup truck turned her way and nodded when their eyes met. It was a friendly enough gesture for this neck of the woods, especially for a First Nations woman walking the highway alone. She was used to these interactions and simply nodded back silently. She hesitated when she reached the door to the station, glancing back at the man who had his back to her. She opened the door and entered.

Inside the station, a pair of local senior citizens were sitting at one of the tables enjoying a coffee and gossiping. The woman was doing most of the talking, while the man nodded and tried to pretend he was not watching the television hanging from the roof nearby above the coffee machines. A young white male in his early twenties sat behind the register, all but ignoring everyone in the store as he flipped through a moto-cross magazine. A news anchor on the television was reading out the midday news as Aiyana crossed the station heading for the snacks aisle.

"And a happy ending to the story of missing toddler Michael Sussex today," the anchor said. "Nat Grady has the story."

Aiyana reached the section of the aisle containing various jerky and pepperoni sticks and started gathering an armload while the news played on in the background.

"Thanks, Alan. Last week we reported the story of young Michael Sussex, only three years old, who had gone missing from his family home after being accidentally left unattended. Today, that story took a turn for the good as young Michael was found early this morning, cold, wet, and terrified, but very much alive."

Aiyana tilted her head, listening to the news as she continued to gather steak bites and jerky.

"Michael was finally located when Daniel McBride, a highway worker with Northern Pavement Limited, was performing brush clearing on some culverts along Cecil Lake Road."

Aiyana reached the limit of what she could carry and started making her way slowly toward the counter, pausing briefly to consider some potato chips but then deciding against them. She approached the counter and started putting down her goods, earning a derisive snort from the clerk for interrupting his magazine reading. He looked at her pile of goods as she continued to place the food on the counter, and picked up a bag of jerky. He waved it at her.

"Feeling a little carnivorous?"

Aiyana froze in the middle of placing a pepperoni stick on the counter and looked at the clerk. Her mute silence made him laugh and he shook the beef jerky pack in her face.

"Oh…" Aiyana shrugged. "Yeah. Sure. I guess."

The clerk rolled his eyes and started scanning all of Aiyana's items. Aiyana's attention drifted to the old couple, now both watching the television in silence, before she too turned her eyes to the news as the picture returned to the anchor in the newsroom.

"Well, we can all breathe a sigh of relief knowing young Michael is home safe and sound."

The anchor tapped a stack of papers on the desk before continuing to the next story.

"In other news, police continue the manhunt for a suspected serial killer in Northern BC. A seventh victim has now been identified in what police are calling a serious targeted attack against First Nations women. So far, police have been unable to identify a suspect in the murders, but a statement by the RCMP released earlier today urges people to stay safe, travel in pairs, and avoid walking the highways at night. If you have any information that could be useful to this investigation, you are urged to contact your local police or to contact Crime Stoppers anonymously."

A finger-snapping sound caused Aiyana to break her attention on the television and return to the clerk. In her trance, while watching the news, she did not realize she had opened a bag of beef jerky and was gnawing on it while staring at the television. The clerk, realizing he had her attention, snapped at her.

"I said that would be forty-two thirty-five… and you can't eat that before you pay for it."

Aiyana nodded and began fishing through the pockets of her long winter coat. She produced a crumpled fifty-dollar bill and handed it to the clerk.

"Are you okay?" the clerk asked as he handed Aiyana her change.

Aiyana realized she had jerky hanging out of her mouth and took it out. Embarrassed, she put the half-eaten piece of meat back in its package and began scooping all of the snacks into her backpack.

"Yeah. Sorry… yes, I'm fine. Just starving is all."

"Uh huh… want anything else?"

Aiyana shook her head as she finished loading her backpack and slung it up on her shoulder. She smiled awkwardly at the clerk and then made her exit from the store. The door made a soft chime as it closed behind her, and the clerk returned to reading his magazine.

"Feed your wild side, weirdo…" he mumbled.

Aiyana walked alone for over an hour heading South on the desolate section of highway between Topley and Topley landing. It was a forty-kilometre stretch of highway that wound its way South-Southwest through the forest with a myriad of spurs leading to logging operations. Every once in a while, a vehicle would approach going the same direction as her, and Aiyana would turn and hold her hand out with her thumb up, a well-known sign to drivers that she was requesting a ride.

Hitchhiking itself in British Columbia was not illegal, but picking up hitchhikers was, so most drivers sauntered right past content to ignore her. In the North, it was a way of life for a lot of people who lived alone or in poverty. For Aiyana, she was a full nomad and lived on the move all the time. Sometimes she was lucky and someone gave her a ride closer to where she was going, even though she never knew where that might be. She never stayed in one area long, just enough to make a bit of money, and then on she went. She avoided big cities and large communities, preferring instead to wander the high-altitude roads of Northern Canada, even in the winter.

A white sedan car approached from behind, and as with every other car, Aiyana turned and held out her outstretched thumb. Almost immediately, the car turned on its left blinker, indicating to other drivers that it was pulling over. Aiyana approached the car as it stopped just ahead of her, and the passenger window rolled down. The driver greeted her with a smile, an unassuming caucasian man in his middle thirties or so with dark hair, and black-rimmed glasses.

"Need a lift?" he asked.

Aiyana lifted her fist and showed the thumbs-up signal she had been using.

"That's the point of this, I figured."

The driver smiled and leaned over, opening the door for her. She swung her backpack off her shoulder and climbed into the passenger seat.

"I'm heading all the way down to Burns Lake. How far do you want to go?"

Aiyana tucked her backpack on the passenger floor between her feet and fixed her seatbelt.

"Burns Lake sounds nice."

"Funny girl…" the driver said under his breath as he put the car in gear.

As they pulled away, Aiyana reached into her backpack and took out a new pack of beef jerky. She tore the package open, her hands trembling ever so slightly, and quickly stuffed a piece of the meat in her mouth. She hoped that maybe her eating might dissuade conversation, but was not shocked in the least when the driver spoke anyway.

"I'm Kevin."

There was a long pause when Aiyana didn't answer. She kept chewing.

"And you are?"

She sighed.

"Aiyana."

"Pleasure to meet you, Aiyana."

Kevin glanced over at his passenger, who still did not answer. She kept chewing and turned her head to the passenger window. At the moment she swallowed, she stuffed a new piece of jerky in her mouth.

"That's a lot of junk food for such a tiny lady… you must be starving."

Aiyana stopped chewing for a moment and looked down at her backpack. Empty wrappers stared back at her. Almost all the food she bought at the station was gone.

"I'm never full these days it seems…" she whispered.

"Well," Kevin began, taking on an almost pompous tone as he pushed the glasses up the bridge of his nose with his finger. "I imagine there *has* to be something better you can eat. That stuff will kill you."

Aiyana looked at him in silence for a moment. When he made eye contact with her and smiled, she simply shrugged and returned to eating what little she had left. For a time, they drove in blessed silence, with Kevin concentrating on the road and Aiyana munching away on her beef jerky. When at last she finished all of it, she sighed and placed the empty package in her backpack with all the others. She closed the bag and sat back in the car. Deciding it was too hot, she unwound the scarf around her neck and placed it in her lap. Kevin looked over.

"Wow!" he said, noticing a giant scar along the side of Aiyana's neck that was previously covered by the scarf. "That's quite a scar! From an accident?"

Aiyana suddenly tensed up and immediately began wrapping the scarf around her neck again.

"I'm sorry… I didn't mean to offend you…"

"It's fine," Aiyana replied as she finished tying the scarf up again. "I just don't like to talk about it."

"No problem. If you're hot, I can turn the air conditioning on or open a window."

Aiyana forced a weak smile.

"Yes please."

"A/C or window?"

"Pardon? Oh. A/C is fine, please."

Kevin reached out and flicked on a dial for the car fan and then turned the dial beside it to the blue side. Immediately, a rush of cool air filled the cab. Aiyana opened her backpack again, rifling through the empty snack bags hoping to find one that was still full.

"You know… all that salt isn't very good for your blood. You should drink something. Do you have anything to drink?"

Aiyana shook her head no and she continued her search in vain.

"There's a bottle of water in the back seat. It's yours… if you want it."

Aiyana paused a moment in her search, deciding that there was indeed no more remaining food. She turned to look in the back seat, and locating the bottle of water, leaned back as far as her seatbelt would allow and retrieved it. Along with the bottle of water in the back, Aiyana noticed a briefcase, a newspaper from Prince George BC, and some folders of what appeared to be business paperwork. She returned to her seat and spun open the lid on the water bottle, taking a long drink from it. Kevin smiled.

"Better?"

"Yes. Thank you. So what's with the briefcase? You a lawyer or something?"

"God no! I'm a real estate agent."

"Oh! That's so much better."

"Ouch! You don't like real estate agents?"

"Doesn't really matter what you do. All people are the same in the end."

"That's pretty deep… are you a counsellor?"

Aiyana withdrew to silence again, her gaze turning to the passenger window.

"Alrighty then…" Kevin said, shaking his head.

Aiyana stared out the window in silence, sipping the water until it was all gone. The trees outside started to blur as they flew past. Her eyes fluttered.

"I don't feel right…" she said, her words slurring.

"What did you… do…"

The world faded to gray as Aiyana's head slumped to her chest. Kevin smiled and pushed his glasses up the bridge of his nose.

********

Aiyana opened her eyes and found herself in a creepy rustic cabin of sorts. Furs and animal trophies adorned the walls of the room. A large wooden bed occupied the center of the space, with the only light coming from an old gas lantern on a wooden bedside table. A single-pane window showed that it was night outside.

Groaning, Aiyana tried to sit up but found herself bound to the bed by what appeared to be old frayed ropes. She realized she was still fully clothed, but had been stripped of her coat and the scarf that was around her neck. The sheets and the pillows on the bed smelled of mildew and dried blood. Just then, Kevin entered the room carrying another lantern. He smiled at Aiyana when he saw she was awake, and hung the lantern from a chain and hook that was dangling from the roof.

"Glad you're awake. I have something to show you."

Kevin held up a rolled leather satchel for Aiyana to see before he moved to the left side of the bed. Aiyana's gaze was fixed on him.

"What's going on?"

Kevin unrolled the leather satchel on the edge of the bed, revealing an array of butcher's tools. There was an assortment of knives with varying blade lengths and shapes, a bone saw, and a ribcage splitter.

"You're a smart girl. I'm sure you can figure it out. Even if you're a transient, you've probably seen the news."

"You're the serial killer everyone is looking for? The highway of tears killer?"

Kevin pauses, his fingers brushing a huge chef's knife in the leather kit.

"I hate that name… it doesn't seem original to me. I mean… there's *already* a highway of tears… did you know that?"

Aiyana showed no emotion.

"You should really let me go…"

Kevin removed the chef's knife from the kit and began to circle the bed like a wolf boxing in its prey.

"Seven hundred and fifty miles of highway… Nineteen official victims. I mean me…"

"Please…"

"… I've been credited with seven kills now. It's more like twelve… because I've become rather good at *disposing* of my toys…"

"Let. Me. Go."

Kevin idly picked dirt from under his fingernails with the tip of the knife. Suddenly he smiled, a childish smile full of glee.

"Hey! Do you want to see my collection?"

Aiyana watched in silence as Kevin practically

skipped across the room. He stopped at a bookshelf and giggled as he retrieved a binder. Slowly he turned, purposely exaggerating his movements as he opened the binder and showed it to her. He walked closer, pointing out things in the binder as he spoke, and flipping pages like a mother showing pictures of her firstborn. As he approached, the light touched the pages, and Aiyana noticed the binder was full of driver's licenses and identification cards, all displayed like hockey cards.

"Some of these I just stole… you know? From purses and such over the years."

Kevin sat on the edge of the bed, displaying the binder like a trophy.

"But the ones on the *first* pages… I took more than their ID. They're very special to me… and look!"

Kevin tapped an empty pouch on the page.

"A place for you!"

"Why…"

"Why?"

Kevin looked genuinely confused.

"Why does there always have to be a why? Why does anyone do the things they do… what makes a man like blondes when another likes men? What makes a girl hitchhike alone when the news says not to? I don't know *why*, Aiyana. Just…"

Kevin stood and closed the binder.

"… because I can."

"Why me?"

"Why you? Because you're my type, Aiyana.

You're my *blonde*."

Kevin laughed a maniacal laugh at his joke as he returned the binder to his shelf. Aiyana turned her attention to the room, and she noticed her backpack on a chair opposite her, beside the door that Kevin had entered through. The backpack was open, and all of her empty food packets were scattered across the floor. She struggled against her bonds, causing Kevin to turn and notice her attention fixed on the backpack.

"Wow. What's the matter? You're *still* hungry?"

Kevin crossed the room and set the knife down on the foot of the bed as he did. He scooped up the backpack and brought it to the left side of the bed.

"We should get to know each other!"

Kevin dumped the contents of her pack on the bed. Almost everything inside it was empty food packs, with a couple of pieces of spare clothing. He began sorting through it, tossing the food wrappers and clothes to the floor. He paused and lifted a single piece of pepperoni still in its package. Aiyana's stomach grumbled.

"Please don't. Let me go! Please!!"

Ensuring he savoured every moment, Kevin opened the pepperoni and scarfed it all down in front of her, laughing while pieces of it fell from his mouth. He tossed the empty pack to the ground and walked back to the chair, grabbing Aiyana's coat which had been bundled up beneath the pack. He violently stuffed his hands into pocket after pocket, becoming increasingly agitated as he did.

"Where is it?" he mumbled.

He threw the coat to the ground.

"Where IS IT!!"

In a rage, he stomped back towards the bed, grabbing the knife and circling to the right side of the bed. He leaned down, brandishing the knife in Aiyana's face and emphasizing her name as he spoke.

"*Aiyana*… you're a bad girl. You shouldn't go anywhere without ID, *Aiyana*. So… let's talk about you now, shall we?"

Kevin teased the tip of the knife along the side of Aiyana's face, moving it ever lower until he paused against the scar on her neck.

"Let's talk about this scar. Tell me… did it hurt?"

A tear rolled down Aiyana's cheek. She was trembling visibly. Kevin seemed to revel in her fear. He stroked the knife tip gently along the length of the scar.

"It's really beautiful. I bet it bled. A lot. Funny thing about scars…"

"Please…" Aiyana's stomach grumbled audibly. "Please let me go."

"… They say it hurts twice as much when you cut one… as if the original wound adds on top of the new one. Let's find out!"

Kevin stared into Aiyana's eyes as he pressed the knife into the flesh on Aiyana's scar.

"Scream… I know you're scared. Show me how much!"

Instead of screaming, Aiyana's body went completely rigid and calm. The pupils in her eyes opened, and she drew a long breath that sounded more like a sigh. Kevin sat up abruptly. He looked at the scar on her neck, now opened wide with an almost five-inch gash from below her ear almost to her clavicle. The skin was parted to muscle, but there was not a single drop of blood.

"What the…"

In an explosion of motion, Aiyana's left arm snapped the bonds that were holding it like they were paper. She seized Kevin's wrist above his fist holding the knife. His face contorted in both surprise and pain, as the grip she had tightened, and the wet crunch of snapping bone filled the room.

"You should have let me go…"

Instinctively, Kevin threw all his weight behind the arm holding the knife, forcing the blade down where it impacted directly with Aiyana's chest. Her grip released and Kevin let go of the knife. He tried to sit up and get off the bed, but Aiyana's right arm broke free of her bonds in a similar fashion as before. She landed an impossibly strong blow to the center of his chest and sent him sailing across the room.

Kevin rolled to his knees on the floor, spitting blood. Across the room, Aiyana sat up. The chef's knife sticking straight up was firmly embedded in her chest. She looked down at the handle of the blade, and with her right hand, slowly drew it out of her body and tossed it towards Kevin. The clean blade clattered on the ground near him, and he looked from the shining knife to the gaping bloodless wounds on her chest and neck.

"What the fuck are you?" Kevin choked through blood and pain.

Aiyana stood from the bed and walked slowly towards the broken man sprawled and bleeding on the floor. Her stomach growled as the scent of blood flooded the room.

"Starving" she replied, cold as ice.

********

Daylight shone in a cloudless sky as Aiyana walked alone down the highway once more, her backpack slung over her shoulder. As before, she stuck out her thumb to passing cars. This time, she did not turn to face the oncoming vehicles, just stuck out her thumb when she heard them approaching. Her gaze was on the horizon, fixed and blank.

A large black pickup truck rolled to a stop alongside her, and the passenger window rolled down. An older First Nations man, with greying hair, a beard, and wearing a plaid jacket, leaned over to speak to Aiyana.

"Hey, lady! You shouldn't be out here alone. Killer on the loose and all that. Hop in, I'll give you a ride. Please?"

Aiyana looked at the man and smiled, nodding. She opened the passenger door and climbed in, setting the backpack at her feet. She was not wearing her scarf.

"What are you doing out here alone?" The old man asked. "You lost?"

"No."

"Something bad happen?"

"No."

They drove in silence for a while, with the driver occasionally looking over at her. He noticed the scar on her neck, now healed back up.

"Helluva scar, that is."

"Yes. It is."

"You don't cover it?"

"Does it bother you?"

"Well... no..." the man said awkwardly. "Just thought it might bother you... people asking about it and all."

"It's okay. I had a scarf, but I lost it."

"Listen..." the old man began. "If you need anything at all, you just let me know. There's some homemade venison jerky in the glovebox there if you're hungry. Just help yourself."

Aiyana smiled and looked out at the woods while they drove.

"Thanks... but I just ate."

# The Touch of Shadow

The bitter chill of approaching winter bit Jacob Turner's cheek as he held his .303 rifle tight to his shoulder. The dusk of coming night blanketed him, like a soft quilt woven by a caring grandmother. His breath rose in wispy streams to dissipate in the waning sunlight. With all the calm and poise he could muster, Jacob waited patiently in the grass, listening with every ounce of his concentration for the sound he had heard. Above him, a gentle breeze rustled the dying leaves of a birch tree.

Jacob cautiously raised his head so he could see above his scope. His rifle rested on a dead pine that he lay behind. About fifty paces beyond his hiding spot, the trees thinned a little, allowing a great view of a marshy clearing that stretched out to a distant tree line. The fading light was hindering Jacob's already limited ability to see what had made the noise he heard, but that did not stop him from scanning the horizon as diligently as an artist appraises his work. In the dusk, he could still pick out movement, but it was confined to the swaying silhouettes of the tall trees all around him. He scrutinized the marsh and the forest floor before him, but the world was a silent black canvas and did not relinquish its secrets.

Finally resigned to having missed what made the sound, Jacob let out a long breath and looked over at his faithful companion Jake. The big Siberian husky simply looked at him with an ear-up, head-askew glance that said he was curious about his owner's obvious tension. Jacob knew that if the dog sensed nothing, then more than likely nothing was there. He reached out with his trigger hand and scratched the dog behind its ears. Jake lapped his warm tongue against Jacob's exposed wrist as he graciously accepted the affection.

"You're right, aren't ya boy? I might just be losing my touch in my old age. There's no deer out there, just my imagination, right?"

Jacob shifted his gaze back to the marsh as he continued to scratch behind the dog's ear. The forest remained still and silent. The dog yawned, bringing Jacob's attention back to it.

Jake was large for a husky, even a male. Sometimes Jacob had wondered if the previous owners had lied about the purity of his breed. Even if they had, it would have been impossible to tell. His markings were beautiful, a distinct mixture of white and black hues in a thick coat that covered powerful muscles. His white eyes shone with brilliance, even in the fading light. There was no more faithful companion to be had out here in the wild. The dog was Jacob's best friend.

For as long as he could remember, Jacob had been hunting these woods. As a child, he often came out with his father and grandfather. They would spend weeks in the summertime charting the migration of the deer and finding the most active game trails for the moment the season would be open. When his grandfather passed away, the act of hunting and simply being in the woods brought Jacob and his father closer together. It was their ritual to hunt. They had never missed a season until the year his father died. That year, and every year since, Jacob had not been to the woods once. Something about them had become hollow to him, almost as though the soul of the woods had aged into the afterlife along with his father.

As time rolled on, however, Jacob began to feel a need to return to the woods again; a beckoning to go where he had once found profound peace. When the season had opened, he packed his rifles, gear, and supplies into his pickup, and headed for the woods once more. This was his first time being out alone though; alone except for his dog and his thoughts.

Jacob laid the rifle down on the ground and rolled

over, resting the back of his head against the log as he looked up at the forest canopy above him. In the breeze, the leaves rustled softly, and some fell slowly to the ground as the shifting season took its toll on the forest. All around him, Jacob could smell the sweet decay of the leaves as the season inexorably marched toward winter. Jacob's gaze slid from the birch above his head to a dying pine a few feet away. As he stared up at the brown needles hanging from the towering tree limbs, he found himself hoping for a long, cold, Canadian winter.

"Sure could use a long winter this year Jake. If something doesn't kill those bugs soon, there won't be much forest left to hunt in."

*Snap.*

Jacob flipped awkwardly onto his stomach and fumbled to get his rifle into a firing position. He pushed his hat back from his bushy grey eyebrows and took up aim. The coatings on his scope made the forest a little easier to see as he scanned the trees and the marsh for the source of the sound. This time he was sure he had heard it. Something was out there, and judging from the game trail and tracks he had spotted earlier, it was a deer. Once more, the forest showed no signs of life. Nothing moved save the gentle sway of the treetops. It never occurred to him, but there was no sound at all save the whisper of the breeze in the trees.

Jacob frowned and blinked a few times. He looked over at Jake. The dog was alert this time, but he was focused on Jacob, not the marsh.

"Didn't you hear it, boy?"

Jake licked Jacob's face and whimpered. Jacob pushed the dog away and wiped the slobber from his bristly beard.

"I am losing it, boy. Come on, let's head for the truck. I'm getting the heebie-jeebies out here."

Jacob went about gathering his gear with no haste at all. It was close to full dark now, and they had a good walk back to the truck. Chastising himself for letting it get so dark, he gathered his lunch kit and placed it in his pack. Next, he pulled up the ground sheet he had been lying on, folded it, and placed it into his pack. He slung the pack over his shoulders and then picked up his rifle and flashlight. He put the light in his pocket, deciding instead to keep what little night vision he had intact for the time being.

"Come on boy, we'll try again tomorrow. Maybe we'll have better luck over by the creek."

Jake trotted ahead into the trees as Jacob began the long hike back to the truck. Jacob watched him stop here and there to sniff at things Jacob could only begin to imagine. He held back from the dog to see if he could still see him from far off. Even in the fading light, the dog's movement was distinguishable against the still background of the forest. He had to assure himself though, and so he held back farther to gauge how long he could track his companion. Jake did not seem to mind and slipped further away without looking back.

*Snap.*

Jacob spun to face the way he had come. Without even realizing it, he had brought the rifle up on aim from his hip. It had sounded as though a twig had broken underfoot. The sound had come from behind him. He scrutinized the darkness, trying with all his might to catch a glimpse of something moving in the shadows. Nothing did.

An icy chill shuddered through Jacob. For the first time in his entire life, he felt exposed in the woods. He had always felt comfortable here in the past. Now he felt as though a stranger had invaded his home. He shivered, even though he felt warm. Slowly, he forced himself to relax. The rifle lowered in his hands, and he let out a sigh. A gust of cold air made the hair at the nape of his neck stand up. The breeze had changed to a wind.

"Get it together man," Jacob said under his breath. "It was probably just a pine-cone from a dead tree."

*Snap.*

It was not a pinecone. This time the rifle did not stop at his hip. He found himself rapidly scanning the forest around him through the piercing view of his scope. The coatings on the lens added an eerie luminescence to the forest. He whipped the barrel of his rifle to and fro, searching the darkness for some sign of threat. He felt an ominous cloud of fear fall over him like the dark billowing of a raging storm cloud. His heart hammered in his chest. His attention was fixed on the trees and the shadows they played along the path toward where he had been.

*Snap.*

Panic welled up in his throat. A million questions began running through his mind. Something was out there, he was now sure of it. Whatever it was seemed to be stalking him. He could not see it; it was invisible in the shadows of the forest, but he was sure beyond doubt that it was there.

"Who's there?" Jacob shouted weakly against the dark.

His wrinkled hands were shaking. He had to blink to try and focus his vision through the scope. Blind terror consumed him. He had never felt this way before. He had heard these same sounds a million times before, but it had always been a deer. This felt like something altogether different. Against whatever it was that was out there, he felt like prey. His grip on the rifle tightened. He was prey with teeth.

*Snap.*

Jacob fell to a knee, futilely attempting to steady his aim. To either side of the trail, shadows seemed to come alive. He blinked to clear his vision and shook his head. He tried to tell himself that his mind was playing tricks, but it did nothing to calm him down. He blinked again, quickly wiping his hand across his brow. There was no sweat. His hand went to his pocket and fumbled for his flashlight. He tried hard to control his shaking.

*Snap.*

It was behind him now. Without thinking he spun and squeezed the trigger. The dark calm of the forest erupted with the violent concussion of the shot as the rifle fired. In that instant, all that was calm was suddenly plunged into chaos. The echoes only made the crack seem louder.

And then it was still again. Silence rushed in to fill the void left by the gunshot. The only sound Jacob could hear was the ringing in his ears. He struggled to gain composure. Nothing made sense. Adrenaline coursed through his veins like liquid fire, making it extremely difficult to recall recent events. Something was amiss, and he had to focus to remember what it was.

There had been the snapping sound. It seemed to be following him. Closer and closer it had been. Suddenly it had been behind him. It filled him with terror that whatever it was had found its way behind him without him knowing. He had spun and fired before thinking about it. There had been another sound though, mixed in with the sound of the shot. It had been familiar, but somehow strange; somehow out of place.

Jacob gingerly felt the ground beneath him for the flashlight that had fallen from his pocket. A new fear gripped him as his fingers found the cold metal shaft of the light. Trembling, he flicked the switch. His heart stopped. The sound had been a yelp.

Jake lay on the trail a few feet from him. He was sprawled out on the ground. Blood matted the left side of his face. He was not moving.

"Jake," Jacob managed to gasp as his rifle fell to the ground. He scrambled towards his dog.

"Jake," he said again, picking the animal's limp form up in his hands. "No…"

In shock, Jacob did not notice a sudden numbness in the fingers of his left hand.

*Snap.*

Jacob whirled around. This time, he had no rifle to aim into the darkness. It lay on the trail near where the sound had come from. He pointed his flashlight into the woods with his right hand, as his left held the dead body of his companion. The numbness spread to his whole hand.

A young boy stood on the trail, not two paces on the other side of Jacob's rifle. The sudden appearance of something so unexpected froze Jacob to the bone. His shuddering stopped. Pure and absolute fear gripped him. The boy just stood there on the trail, not moving, not smiling, and not speaking. His clothes were dark, almost all black save a few scattered designs. He wore black cargo pants low on his waist, the band of his underwear rimming his waist above his pant line. A sweater, unzipped in the front and with the hood pulled up, hung limply from his shoulders. His face was shrouded in shadow.

Jacob could do nothing more than stare with his eyes wide and his mouth hanging open. He could barely take a breath. The boy took a step forward. His mouth opened, and the voice that ushered forth made the hair on Jacob's neck stand on end.

"You shot your dog," the boy said, his voice like a moaning whisper and a piercing howl, all rolled into one.

Jacob said nothing. He dropped Jake's body back to the ground and shook his hand. His whole left side was numb. His right hand started to shake again.

The boy took another step forward. The beam from the flashlight pierced the shrouded veil of darkness that lay across the boy's face. Where his eyes should be, gaping holes into nothing stared back, a shadow that the light could not touch.

Jacob clutched his hand to his chest, dropping the flashlight to the ground. He stared open-mouthed at the ground, where the body of his closest friend lay. He could not pull his breath against the racking pain in his chest.

The boy stepped closer, a ghost made of shadow.

"What… are… you?" Jacob managed with the last of his breath.

As the boy stepped beside Jacob, he reached his hand out and touched Jacob's shoulder. The boy spoke into the silence, his voice like howling wind over thunder, as the world fell to blackness darker than the night.

"I think you know."


In the woods, on a trail meant for animals, a deer comes upon the crumpled bodies of a man and his dog. Cautiously it approaches, unsure of any danger.

Nearby, a pinecone falls from a dead tree, shaken loose by the wind. As it hits the ground, the deer darts off into the woods.

*Snap.*

# SEVEN TURNS OF THE SCREW

Thirty-seven steps. Able Seaman Nigel Remner had counted it out many times during his downtime while the ship was ashore. He had heard the tales about sea training exercises from his more experienced shipmates and felt mentally prepared for the exertion. Alarms waking you from sleep. Action stations at all hours of the day and night. Drills you responded to as if they were real, over and again until muscle memory took over. He knew it was thirty-seven steps from his bunk to the door of his mess because he had paced it out.

The sea training was not the only thing on his mind these last few days since leaving port, however. This was his first time sailing on a Navy vessel, and his shipmates had been threatening a hazing for all the green apples. That was the name they gave first-time sailors. They called it 'seven days, or seven turns of the screw,' and very very little information on the ceremony was shared with those who would undertake it. Every time seven days or seven turns were mentioned, it was met with giggles and guffaws from veteran shipmates. The more questions green apples would ask, the more aloof and ambiguous the answers became.

Sometimes, a particular veteran or another might drop an anecdote or other story about things they had seen during the hazing. None of them sounded especially harmful to the body. More harm to one's pride, than anything. Especially having your eyebrows shaved off while tied to a post with duct tape.

Nigel had wanted to be a sailor most of his life, so he was willing to do anything to earn his shipmates' respect. He met every veiled threat as an intention to get a rise out of him or shake him up, and so his default response became 'bring it on.' Today was day six, and the day was ending.

Nigel laid on his back in his small rack. He looked up at the metal ceiling, which was also the bottom of the bunk above him. He had taped pictures of his family there to keep him company while deployed. There was also a poster of his favourite motorcycle, one he hoped to save money for and buy someday. The mattress he was on was stiff, but somehow strangely comfortable. It was barely the size of a single bed, narrower but a tad longer to accommodate taller people. Height was not a gift Nigel possessed.

He had a youthful frame, energetic and not yet filled in by young adult muscle. He was gainly and quite thin, which made him a prime target for a lot of chiding from his seniors. His energy and enthusiasm were magnetic though, and he felt like he had made a lot of friends already in his time aboard.

Lights out had happened nearly two hours ago, so the mess was dark. Darker still because Nigel had drawn closed the cloth curtain that afforded him what little privacy could be had in a mess. Faint red light teased its way into the darkness, seeping through the cracks of the mess door from the hallways outside. After lights out, the ship would turn off all white lights and illuminate passageways only with red. It took some getting used to, but the reason was red light did not impact a person's night vision the same way white light did. Nigel had not yet had much chance to test that for himself.

The ship had left port on a Monday morning, nearly on the dot at eight o'clock AM, heading straight for the South Pacific to rendezvous with a battle group for exercises. Nigel was apprehensive about his first sailing but wildly excited also. His great-grandfather had been a merchant marine during World War two and had kept a detailed journal. Nigel had grown up on stories of Saint Elmo's Fire, the magic of sunsets at sea, midnight algae blooms under the stars, and the violence of ocean storms. Every trip off the dock teased adventure Nigel yearned for, and so the needle between trepidation and excitement had swung deep into the latter in short order. He kept a mental record as the ship slipped its lines and the tug took it out. He memorized the song of the seagulls, the smell of the salt air, the sunlit cloudless sky, and the sounds of the crew and engines. He would write his own journal someday, in the hopes that it would inspire some future generation of Remners to sail themselves.

As the thought of that first day, and the five more that followed, played in his mind like a movie, Nigel rolled onto his side. His eyes were fixed on the blackness in his rack and the faint, almost indiscernible glow of the hallway lights. He listened to the symphony of snoring and deep breathing from the men who slept in his mess. Together with the sounds of the filtered air system, fans, distant machinery, and the whooshing of water against the steel hull, it all came together into a white noise like no other. He remembered how the first few nights, he barely slept at all, and now only six days into his first sail, he couldn't imagine ever sleeping in silence again.

Thirty-seven steps. Again, he thought of the pacing between his bunk and the door. An itch made him rub his legs against the mattress. During sea training exercises, it was quite common for sailors to sleep in their uniforms. The practice shaved moments off your response time to incidents, his shipmates had told him. The fire-retardant cloth of the uniform was not the most comfortable to sleep in, and Nigel found his thighs and calves itchy often. At least they had laundry services, so it was a clean uniform every day. Still, though, Nigel found he had to reach down and scratch the itch on his left shin. Rubbing against the mattress was not quite helping. They had said tomorrow the sea training exercises were to start in earnest. Coupled with tomorrow being the seventh day, Nigel was overflowing with anticipation. He imagined there was not going to be much sleep for him tonight.

Thirty-seven steps, he thought to himself, picturing in his mind's eye how he would slide the curtain open and leap out of the rack at the first sound of an alarm. He thought of where exactly his boots were on the floor below him, and how he would step into them and rip the side-zipper up. He thought of how he would have to make way for Benedict who slept in the bunk below him to get out of his rack, and Jeppardini from the rack above. He ran through his mind where he needed to go once he made it out of his mess.

*Straight aft to the two-deck ladder. Drop down to three-deck. Go aft past the mess hall, past the galley. Keep going past stores and the ship's office. All the way to the after ladder, back up to three-deck. Straight aft to the hangar ladder. Up to one deck, and aft to the hangar. Get into bunker gear. Grab my first aid kit. Report in and await orders.*

It was a lot to remember in only six days. A veteran sailor named Quinton Paule had told Nigel he had been aboard a ship that caught fire for real once. Before that day, Paule hated all the training too. He thought they did it too much. Exercise fatigue, he used to call it. But on the day the fire broke out, and 'no duff' was declared at the end of the alarm signalling a true emergency, Paule said his body reacted without conscious thought. The fire was extinguished methodically and safely, and almost no one was hurt save a couple of cases of heat exhaustion. Since that day, Paule welcomed every exercise and even advocated for more. Repetition, he said, won the day that day. The value of excessive practice would never again be questioned in his career.

It was nearly an hour that passed that way, with Nigel occasionally scratching his shin and running through his duties in his mind. Nearly an hour before sleep finally blessed him, and his snoring added to the song of the mess. The ship tilted and swayed as it crossed swells on the ocean. Like a cradle, lulling all the babies onboard to a restful sleep.

*******

Nigel's eyes slid open and blinked a few times. He stretched out in his rack, accidentally hitting the metal wall at his back. The sound startled him, it was so loud, and immediately he froze to make sure he had not woken any of his shipmates. He strained to listen in the darkness, but he heard nothing. The ship was silent and seemed to have stopped moving. Then a wave of panic washed over him. *The ship was silent.*

His breath shallow, Nigel rolled onto his back and lay still as he could. He listened intently for any sign of alarm, recalling something Jeppardini had told him over dinner a day past.

"You'll know before an alarm comes," he had said. "There'll be signs. For example, for most exercises, the first thing they do is crash ventilation to isolate fire or smoke or whatever. When that happens, you'll know. After a few days at sea, there's nothing quite like that kind of silence."

Nigel knew exactly what Jeppardini had meant. After six days of forced air circulation, fans, and all the other noise, it was entirely alien to suddenly hear nothing. He quickly pulled back his curtain, getting ready to vault out of bed in advance of the alarm.

The mess was still dark, and the little trickle of red hallway light was still seeping through the door frame. It was enough to see, so Nigel slipped into his boots and zipped them up. He stole a glance at Benedict and Jeppardini's racks and noticed that their curtains were open and the bunks were empty. He made his way through the rest of the mess, realizing that all of them were empty. A new fear rose in his chest. Had he slept through the alarm? Was the ship already at action stations without him?

Fear beginning to grip him, Nigel stumbled toward the mess door and ripped it open. The red light in the hallways was bright enough to hurt his eyes for a moment, and he shielded his face with his arm. Silence. He looked left and right down the corridor, and then peered around the corner. No one. Just empty halls and red lights. The ship did not even feel like it was moving.

"What the hell…" Nigel breathed, before making his way toward his action stations regardless. The thought occurred to him as he passed through bulkhead doors only to find more empty ship, that this might be the hazing. Pretty elaborate ruse, he thought to himself, if that was what was happening. Was that even possible, he wondered. Would the whole ship be in on a hazing like that?

Nigel found the two-deck ladder and put his hands on the cold steel. Normally, there was a vibration that could be felt on the ladder. It was as absent as the drone of ventilation. Dropping to the third deck, Nigel found more empty corridors. More red light. More silence. As he made his way further aft, he passed the mess hall. The door was open so he stole a peek inside. The room was empty, a few cans of open beer on the table. One bag of chips, half spilled on the carpet. The occupants left in a hurry. The television flickered a soundless movie. Mark Wahlberg's 'Shooter.' That movie seemed to be the only one on the ship.

A peek into the cafeteria as he passed revealed more of the same, while at the same time only deepening the mystery. A couple of plates of half-eaten food. Not a single sign of life. Nigel half expected some angry chief to jump around a corner at any moment, screaming at him for sleeping through the alarms. But every step he took met only more silence. More emptiness.

The door to the stores office was still locked, as it had been when they ended their work day the day before. Nigel shook his head and climbed up the ladder back to the after end of two-deck. The feeling of being alone on the ship was becoming overwhelming, and his footsteps were becoming harder. He felt like he was underwater. Anticipation of the trouble he was in was invading his mind. Yet he pressed on, checking rooms and listening to the silence with rapt attention hoping to hear something. *Anything.* But there was nothing. Absolute quiet. Not even the sloshing of water against the hull. Not a battery whine, a hiss of air, or a rumble of engines and generators. Complete and total emptiness.

Nigel finally reached the final ladder to climb to his post and started up it but stopped. The bridge. There *had* to be someone on the bridge. Maybe it was worth the trouble he would be in, to go and find out what was happening. While the ship was at sea, the two places where people could be found twenty-four hours a day were the bridge and the operations room.

Instead of climbing to the Hangar, he made his way forward and up to the operations room. He knocked on the door and waited. No answer. Frowning, he reached out and pressed the button. The buzzer sounded distantly inside the room. No answer. He tried to open the door but found it locked.

"Okay… what the actual…"

Out of the corner of his eye, he thought he saw a shape move in the dim red light. He strained his eyes, squinting to see.

"Hello? Anyone there?"

No answer. Nigel started to breathe heavily. If this was his hazing, God as his witness, it was working. For a moment, he even questioned why he would stay in the Navy after something like this. Had he drawn the ire of his *entire* ship by his bullish challenge to their teasing? They could not all be on it, could they? There were three hundred people on board this ship. Surely some of them were above this kind of thing.

Nigel crept to where he thought he saw the shadow and leaned around the corner. It was a short passageway leading to a command and control room where processors for the radar systems were kept. There was a closed door directly ahead of him. Three stealthy steps brought him right up against the door, and he pressed his ear against it. Hearing nothing, he slowly opened the door and peered inside the room. The bank of processors stood alone in their space, separated by a foot or two to allow for airflow. Coils of hundreds of cables flowed out of the towers and up into trays where they wound their way around the room, joined by yet more cable, until it ran like a highway of snakes through the bulkhead and into the operations room.

Nigel entered the room, letting the door close silently behind him. He was determined that he was going to spring the trap on whoever it was he saw. Like a hunting cat, he crept through the room, looking into every dark space between the cabinets until he reached the back of the space. He was alone in the room. His heart hammered in his chest, giving him at least *something* he could listen to. He turned to leave and as he did, he saw the door close. Had he not closed it all the way when he came in? Did someone sneak around behind him?

He ran now and tore through the door completely intending to end this charade. His momentum carried him back out to the main hall by the operations room door, and he shot his glance down the corridor and up the ladder. His fist pounded against the locked operations room door.

"Enough! This isn't funny anymore!"

His chest heaved with the weight of his anger. Still, there was no answer. He had reached the limit of his patience. This had gone too far, and they had to know it. Nigel vaulted the stairs to the command deck and flew through the final corridor to the bridge hatch like a guided missile. The hatch was open. And for the third time that night, Nigel's blood went cold. Through the open door, he saw an empty bridge, bathed in the cool blue light of the sun just beginning to pierce the horizon.

Not a prank. Something was wrong. Had to be. The bridge is never unattended at sea. Ever. Did the crew abandon the ship and forget about him? What the *hell* would have caused that? Nigel's mind was in shambles as he stepped onto the bridge. Weakness in his legs threatened to topple him, and he grasped the navigator's chart table to steady himself. Far off near the horizon on the starboard side, a storm could be seen, its dark clouds a stain against the brightening sky, and its sheets of heavy rain like a curtain closing off part of the horizon. The ocean was calm as a lake aside from that.

Like a mouse traumatized by a cat, Nigel made his way to the front of the bridge. He gasped for air through his shocked lungs. There was no answer for what was happening. It was far too elaborate for a hazing. Too against protocol to explain an emergency exercise. The only explanation he could fathom was an abandoned ship, but why? And why leave him behind? Nigel reached the front of the bridge and his hand slapped against the glass of the bridge window, steadying his weak legs.

Faintly outlined by the rising sun, Nigel saw the hulls of the other ships in the battle group. Two destroyers, another frigate like his, and an aircraft carrier sat adrift in the sea together. In the dim light, Nigel squinted to see if there was movement on any of them, but the light was simply too dark yet to make them out. They were too far away. Remembering that bridge watch kept night vision goggles for scanning the horizon at night, Nigel turned and began searching for some. He found a pair locked in a box near the bridge wing doors and took them. Stepping out on the port bridge wing, Nigel lifted the night vision goggles to his eyes and turned them on.

The flash of bright green light physically hurt, and Nigel almost dropped the binoculars over the edge. It was too dark to see the other ships with the naked eye, but too light for the night vision goggles to be any help. Fighting back tears, Nigel leaned against the bridge railing. He wished for home. He thought he was ready for everything people told him he would experience out here, but he was not ready for this. He was miles away from home, surrounded by a void of empty ocean, suspended above yet more miles of unforgiving depths, and utterly alone. He lost his battle against tears and weak knees and dropped to the deck.

Thunder rumbled in the storm far away, booming across the ocean, but when it reached him it sounded like the grumble of a hungry stomach. Though it was nice to finally hear something other than himself, the storm brought him little comfort. He was a logistician. There was nothing he could do to sail the ship alone. He was trapped. Insanity began to gnaw at the back of his mind as he thought about how long he could live on the rations in the fridges. He thought about how long it might take someone to rescue him if he could only send a message. A message. *The radio!*

His sense of purpose renewed, and Nigel leapt to his feet and shot to the communicator station beside the chart table. He picked up the radio microphone and keyed it, not realizing the system was set to the ship's intercom.

"Hello?" he called out. "Can anyone hear me? This is able seaman Nigel Remner. I'm alone on the ship. Something has happened. I need help, over!"

There was no answer save the echo of his voice in the corridors behind him.

"Fuck!" He roared, smashing his fist against the table. He looked everywhere for a switch or something that indicated external communications but he had only been on the bridge twice and that was for tours. He had no idea what he was doing. His fear became rage, and he smashed the microphone to pieces against the chart table.

"Come look at the storm" came a soft voice.

Nigel stopped.

"What? Hello? Who said that!!"

"Come. Come look at the storm."

Nigel searched the corridor behind him, and then he stuck his head out onto the port wing again. He saw no one.

"Where…" Nigel began as he stepped back onto the bridge, but then stopped. On the other side of the ship, out on the starboard bridge wing, stood an officer. Only the left shoulder and arm could be seen, their rank indicated by the epaulet on the shoulder of their uniform. Their hand rested gently on the railing of the bridge wing.

Cautious, and teeming with emotions that blended rage with confusion and fear, Nigel made his way across the bridge.

"Sir? Ma'am?" Nigel squeaked. "What is

happening? The ship is empty. I don't know where I'm supposed to be. I'm so confused."

The officer stood motionless. Their voice came soft and relaxed, in a tone almost awed.

"You're supposed to be here. Right here. Come. Watch the storm."

Nigel stepped through the bridge wing hatch, his eyes locked on the officer. As he stepped out, he noticed the bridge wing was full of people. All silently staring off into the distance. None moving. Nigel swallowed hard, unsure if he should approach. The whole ship *was* in on the hazing. They had to be.

"Sir… is this… is this seven days, seven turns of the screw?"

None of the crew said a word or reacted to him. He leaned past them a bit and looked down the length of the ship on the port side. He saw the entire crew, all three hundred people, lining the upper decks similarly. None moving. All simply staring off into the distance in silence. His gaze came back to the officer as Nigel approached the railing.

"Sir… please… if this is part of the hazing, I'm done. Please stop. I've had enough. I want to go home." The word home choked in Nigel's throat; both because he longed for home more than anything, but also because as he finally reached the railing he had his first look at the officer's face.

Nigel recognized the officer from his time aboard the ship. They had never been formally introduced, but he had known him in passing. Lieutenant Casca was a MARS Officer, usually responsible for piloting and fighting the ship. He was a nice enough guy as the stories went. He had been in the storing line only a few positions from Nigel while they brought supplies on board before the sail. Nigel remembered him laughing and joking with the crew as they passed boxes of potatoes down a human conveyor chain. Now, he was standing motionless on the bridge wing, his eyes staring off to the horizon.

His eyes. Nigel blinked and rubbed his own to make sure the night vision had not done something to his vision. Lieutenant Casca's eyes were silver in their entirety, shining like a polished chrome surface. The skin of his face surrounding his eyes, the bridge of his nose, underneath his eyebrows, and even his forehead was undulating. Moving in ripples like the swell of the ocean. Nigel fell backward against the railing. Lieutenant Casca ignored him.

One by one, the crew members silently climbed the railing and threw themselves overboard into the ocean. Nigel felt sick to his stomach. He knew now there was no way this could be a prank. His mind lurched within itself, reality coming apart at the seams like a cotton shirt in an acid bath. *Splash. Splash. Splash.*

The sound of the crew members hitting the surface of the water some thirty feet below was like artillery shells raining on a battlefield. Nigel thought of his grandfather's journal. Nothing existed in it that was anything like this. Was it chemical warfare? What about the other ships? Before he was aware of it,

Nigel had run through the bridge back to the port side and slammed against the railing. He squinted his eyes and stared at the nearest ship. The aircraft carrier. A gag caught in his throat. Barely visible white specks appeared and vanished at the waterline against the carrier's hull. Splashes. As he realized the carrier's crew was also throwing themselves to the sea, Nigel threw up over the ship's edge.

The bile in his throat was sour and tasted vaguely of mushrooms and metal. Somewhere in his torment, he thought that should be symbolic, but the thought vanished as fast as it came. He collapsed to a sobbing heap on the metal deck. Lieutenant Casca stood as a sentinel across the bridge, still unmoving, still staring out to sea.

"Come watch the storm."

What did Casca mean by that? Why did he keep saying it? Nigel needed answers. He deserved that much. The phrase had become a siren's call in the stark loneliness and raving lunacy of what was happening, and he yearned to grasp some semblance of sanity. They owed him answers.

Nigel rose, and with grand effort as though climbing a steep wet hell while utterly exhausted, he crossed the bridge once more. He stood beside Casca, looking at his metallic eyes and shifting skin. Casca's mouth moved.

"Watch the storm."

With that, Casca climbed the railing and fell over. It was an awkward fall, like a dummy being tipped over a railing. The splash was a sickening thud; the sound of meat hitting the water. Nigel cried freely. His dreams flashed before him and then were gone. There was no journal to write. No legacy to leave. No homecoming. There were just seven days at sea. Seven turns of the screw. He drew a deep breath and then turned his eyes to the horizon. The last sight he saw was a massive dark shape in the storm clouds. Unfathomable. Ancient. Enormous.

And then he stepped over the edge and fell.

# THE JOURNEY

They were a motley crew. A smattering of personalities and backgrounds that should not have enjoyed the company of one another in those days. Yet there they were, lounging about on any surface they could find comfort, reminiscing about the land and lives behind them, and dreaming aloud about that which lay before them. As the vessel swayed onward across waves none of them could see, they chattered on.

There was Philbert Huxley, inventor and historian, a scholar in every sense of the term. He wore odd boots with tall heels, making his lanky frame seem even taller, as though he sought to soak his bow tie among the clouds. Beside him on a fabric-topped counter lay Heinrich Zeisberger, a German industrialist with a gambling addiction, now devoid of all his wealth including his shoes. Near Heinrich, tucked into the corner of the counter against the wall was Nate Smith, one of a pair of young American brothers. They were descendants of farmers in the South of the USA. Somewhere in Northern Texas. Nate's brother Ben sat in an alcove above the counter, his feet dangling so near Nate's head that should Ben fall, the footprint would paint the young boy's cheek. Beside Ben sat Freida Matuga, a Ukrainian housewife with a stern countenance and unhealthy relationship with her odd son Rudo, whose fascination with Nate bordered on suspicion.

Of all the occupants in the cabin though, Zhao Yun Li was the odd man out. Hailing from the Yuan province of China, he was a quiet well-spoken merchant, with the countenance and wisdom of a monk. He travelled with an Irish woman by the name of Neave O'Byrne and her Jack Russel terrier Leprechaun. They rarely spoke to one another. Neave rarely spoke at all beyond grunts and scoffs at the conversations of the others. Leprechaun was never allowed to leave her lap, even when Nate had first arrived and offered to play with him. Neave had only held the dog tighter and glared, prompting Zhao to comment that some people have trouble releasing that which they hold most dear, even if only for short times.

Zhao and Neave had been the first passengers in the cabin when the others had started to trickle in. The brothers had come next, followed by Freida and

Rudo, then Heinrich and Philbert. Pleasantries had been exchanged, some curious questions asked, and then all had agreed that there was simply no more room on the ship to rest for the voyage, and so they had resigned themselves to their smelting pot of worldly experiences and personalities. For a time the conversations were gentle and exploratory. Where do you hail from? What do you do? What is your plan when you reach the New World? Answers and names had been shared, all peacefully, and with the exception of Neave who was introduced by Zhao, all had been courteous. Eventually, as often occurs to people on long trips, the conversation was overtaken by sullen silence.

Heinrich softly snored away curled up on the countertop, his shoe-less feet warmed by woollen socks, and his legs and arms tucked up and crossed. Beside him, Philbert fidgeted with the fabric of his trousers and stared off into space, no doubt percolating some new great technology within his sombre silence. Rudo leaned over to look down at Nate below him, who absently chewed at the reed on a flute he was not playing. Freida had somehow managed to fall asleep sitting up in a posture that telegraphed her history of wealth, and her hand was draped in her son's lap as it had been since she sat down. Ben swung his feet in silence and his eyes darted around the room. It was a vain attempt to pretend he wasn't amused by the questionable placement of Freida's hand.

Neave was idly petting at the fur on Leprechaun's back, who had long ago fallen into that still slumber that dogs are wont to do. Zhao hummed to himself as the boat swayed, smoking from his long pipe. Neave shot him a sideways glance and then looked away sharply. She tried to look at details on the wall, a scratch here, faded paint there. Anything to take her mind away to somewhere else. She found herself making eye contact with Zhao again, who smiled at her while puffing smoke out through his yellowed teeth. His face told a story of age and wisdom; almost as though each wrinkle on his cheeks, brow, and around his eyes represented the parchment teachings of an age. His dark black eyes sparkled with an ease that somehow made Neave uncomfortable, so she sharply turned away once more. Philbert had noticed her and their eyes met for a moment before his awkward smile made her scoff in derision and look down to Leprechaun curled up in her lap. The dog kicked a bit in his dream, settled deeper into her lap, and continued with his nap unabated. Philbert got the message and turned his attention to Zhao.

"Zhao my good chap," Philbert began in his thick British accent. "Have you made this trip before? Any idea the time it will take?"

Zhao laughed a deep chuckle. Thick smoke billowed from his mouth and into his eyes, causing him to waft it away with his free hand.

"No. I have not taken this trip before. As with all of you, this is my first and final journey."

Philbert blinked and Neave scoffed again, pretending to ignore the old Asian.

"What an odd thing to say…" Philbert said, sitting up on the edge of the counter. Ben looked from Zhao to Philbert and back again, then down to his brother Nate who looked up to make eye contact. A quick shrug meant neither of them got the meaning either.

"Odd?" asked Zhao before inhaling deeply from his pipe. His words came forward as though they were shaped by the smoke he exhaled. "Not odd at all. Factual! I have seen that which you all have not accepted what you will not, and come to peace with it. I care not how long the journey will take. I enjoy the time I have to take it!"

Zhao finished with a flourish that swept the smoke from his pipe into a river of mist in the air. It hung like a haze with peeks and valleys, and for a moment, Ben thought he saw green trees and blue waters within the smoke. He squinted but found the image was gone.

Philbert leaned back against the wall and sighed.

"You speak in riddles, good sir."

The room fell silent again, until Rudo, still leaning forward to look down at Nate finally spoke. His accent was thick, but his English was perfect.

"Do you play?"

There was no answer.

"Do you play?" he asked again.

Nate looked up at Rudo, realizing the question was addressed to him.

"Hrm? Oh. Naw. Not really. Of'times I do if'n the mood strikes, but I ain't no good."

Rudo smiled.

"I like the flute. It's pretty."

Freida, who had not been sleeping at all this entire time, slapped the hand that was in Rudo's lap into his crotch. Not enough to hurt, but enough to startle the young man.

"Hush now," she said. "Mom is trying to sleep."

Rudo lowered his head and sank back into the alcove in silence. Ben's eyes darted around the room wondering if anyone else had noticed what Freida had done to her son. No one else seemed to have reacted. Suddenly Heinrich burst from his slumber with a scream, startling everyone except Zhao. Leprechaun barked a few times before Neave was able to shush him.

"Jesus Mary n' Joseph..." Ben said, holding his hand to his chest. "You purt near gave me a heart attack!"

Philbert adjusted his coat and sat back down on the counter as Heinrich attempted to get his bearings.

"I must agree with the American, good sir. What an awful fright that was! Whatever in the world were you dreaming about?"

Heinrich blinked a few times, looking intensely confused as he sat down.

"I was falling..." he began, stopping halfway through and seeming to become even more confused. "And then I hit the ground. How?"

He paused.

"How am I understanding you all? Do you all speak German?"

Philbert and the American boys laughed.

"You are speaking the Queen's English, my boy! How do you not know that?"

Heinrich looked from Philbert to Nate and Ben who nodded confirmation.

"That's as good English as I've heard yet, Heinrich. You been speakin' it since y'all came in this cabin. You don't remember?"

Heinrich's face went white.

"I don't know English. I've never known it."

Nate laughed out loud, drawing haughty looks from both Neave and Freida, who had now seemingly decided she was invested in the conversation.

"Well unless all of us have suddenly learned the German tongue, you sir, are speaking English just fine."

Freida scoffed and turned to her son, leaning so close that she could have been kissing him.

"We are in a cabin of fools it would seem, my love."

Ben hopped down from the alcove, no longer able to stand the odd relationship the two Hungarians had with one another.

"It ain't right to be callin' any stranger a fool who don't deserve it ma'am..." he began as he turned toward Freida and Rudo. "And whatever you're doing with that boy ain't right for no mother and son neither."

Freida's face was white.

"How…" she whispered, swallowing and gulping air. "How do you understand me? How do I understand YOU?"

Zhao laughed again, his pipe adding to the smoke environment hanging in the air.

"Do you not see?" he began again, flourishing his pipe and hands through the air. "Do you not yet know the answers you seek are buried in the questions?"

"Fuck you!" Neave spat. The room fell to silence, shocked to hear her thick Irish voice utter such harsh words. "Ye crazy old bastard. Jus' shut ye damn piehole. Are none o' us here Dead. Ye hear me? None!"

The whole room looked at Zhao, who wore only his usual calm smile, buried under his ancient-looking features.

"Dead?" Philbert shook his head. "Dead? What in the blazes do you mean, woman?"

Neave sat back into her chair and composed herself, petting Leprechaun who was now wide awake and looking as though he wanted to play.

"'Fore ye all arrived, was just me and Zhao here. The crazy ole man was spoutin' nonsense 'bout us all bein' dead. That this…" she waved a hand to indicate the boat. "Is the Ferryman's vessel."

"Chiron?" Philbert asked. "Chiron… the Ferryman who transports souls to the underworld across the river of Styx?"

Neave only shrugged.

"Wait wait wait…" Philbert stood, his gangly height nearly brushing his head against the ceiling. "You mean to tell me, two American boys, a Ukrainian mother and son, a German merchant, an Irish lady, a Chinese… whatever you are… and myself an English inventor, are all somehow dead and sailing together on the boat of a mythological Ferryman to the Greek underworld?"

The room fell silent as Philbert's eyes locked with each of them individually. Zhao simply smiled, silently inhaling from his pipe.

Then the room erupted in laughter. They pounded fists against walls and counters. Held one another. Wiped tears from their faces.

All but Zhao. Zhao smiled and smoked his pipe, feeling the sway of the boat, listening to their laughter. He turned his eyes upwards, still smiling, and focused on something beyond the ceiling boards. Something only he could see. Something only he was ready for.

On the deck above, under a gray and cloudy sky, the Ferryman stood ominous and silent. A sentinel captain, his cloak and robes whipping in the wind like shadow brought to life. In his hand, he flipped a set of gold coins.

Zhao smiled. It was the secret only he knew. He had lived a long life. A full life. This was time for him to enjoy the last journey.

# THE ENGINEERS NIGHTMARE

I could smell the smoke before I knew there was a fire, even from inside the mansion. It was the distant sound of shouting that drew my gaze up from my studies. Something outside was horribly wrong. I left my desk calmly and strode to the library windows just outside my office. The grounds of the De'Ghova estate were alive with activity. Men were running towards the orchard tree line, where they met a wave of servants and children fleeing in the opposite direction. A thick black plume of smoke rose skyward from beyond the trees. The servant's quarters.

Before my mind could catch up to my body, an instinctive reaction had me bolting across the estate lawn like a bullet heading for the tree line and the dark, rolling smoke tower building towards the heavens. I vaguely recalled voices shouting my name as I crashed into the orchard like a tidal wave against a rocky shore. Branches whipped and stung my face as I plunged through the trees. Something in the shouts of the men registered in my mind, telling me I was off the path meant for travelling through the orchards, but I was making a path to the quarters as straight as a crossbow dart and as fast as my feet could carry me. Only one thought sat on the throne of my mind.

*By the Guardians don't let her be inside the house.*

The sight that greeted me when I broke through the other side of the orchard nearly stopped my heart. The huge servant's quarter building was almost completely consumed by fire. Women and children still managed to trickle from whatever exit they could find, immediately set upon by rescuers trying to get survivors away from the flames. I scanned the crowd, hoping to find someone who might know where she was. I noticed a man, badly burned, lying a short distance from me being tended to by a medic. Other victims were being cared for nearby by other medics, and even the veterinarians who normally cared for the horses. The screams of pain, shouts of orders, and the roar of the fire combined into a symphony of sound conducted by Chaos himself. Finally, I set eyes upon the senior baker, sitting alone and adorned in the remains of his scorched clothing. In the span of a breath, I was kneeling beside him.

"Horus! Tell me she got out. Tell me she's not still in there!"

The man blinked at me and shook his head like he was just waking from a deep sleep. His eyes were glazed, but when they met mine directly, recognition dawned within them.

"Young master! Leora… last I saw of her… she was trapped in the kitchen! The fire… it was so hot… so… hot…"

Horus' eyes had glazed over again. My blood froze to ice in my veins as his words sunk in. I felt as though I had been plunged under water. Sound, sight, touch; all of my senses had instantly dulled. Emotional trauma had successfully stolen my soul from the world, and I was now on the outside of life looking in. I could see everything with crystal clarity, from the flames on the roof licking into the jet-black plume of smoke, to the helpless rescuers and bystanders. I swayed side to side, a lonely boat lost on a dark ocean in a storm. Suddenly there was a clap like the strike of lightning, and reality cascaded in on me once more.

"Get ahold of yourself Master De'Ghova! Have you lost your mind?"

A man had a firm grip on my upper left arm. I looked into his face as clarity returned to my thoughts. My cheek stung, but more than that, I could feel the heat from the burning building searing my flesh like the midday sun at its summer peak. I had been wandering towards the flames, but this man, a palace guard, had dared to slap some sense into the master of the house's son. I owed him my life. At that exact moment, as I opened my mouth to thank him, I heard her scream. The sound of her voice issued in peril was like a thunderbolt speared directly into my heart. The ice in my veins became fire.

"Leora!" I screamed, searching the house for any sign of her.

"Lucius!"

I tore off after the sound of her voice, the palace guard close on my heels. We rounded the corner of the building like arrows arching at the apex of their flight. Ahead I saw the canted doors that led down to the storage cellar. I stopped before them and called her name again. The answer came from below, on the other side of the cellar doors.

My bare hands grasped the chains that bolted the cellar doors closed. Bellowing in desperation, I somehow managed to tear the chains from the wooden door. The guard and I threw open the double doors and dove into the darkness below the raging inferno.

Smoke rolled along the roof like river rapids that chose to disobey gravity. The only light in the passageway to the cellar came from flames above through holes that the fire had chewed in the roof. When at last I set my eyes open her, I felt a wave of both relief and panic wash over me.

"Lucius! I'm trapped! I can't open the door."

Seeing her tears and hearing the desperation in her voice nearly stopped my heart. I was only eighteen, and still in full-time study, but if I knew one thing in this forsaken world it was that I wanted to spend my life with her by my side.

"Stand back!" I commanded. "We're going to try and tear the door down."

Still coming off the high of tearing the chain from the cellar doors, I felt as though I could move mountains. The heavy wood and metal door couldn't be any harder to break than a chain. As I grabbed onto the bars and heaved with all my might, the palace guard grabbed a stick and tried to assist me by prying the door open. Leora whimpered behind the door. My hands, sweaty and desperate, slipped from the bars. Still, I refused to give up. Above me, I began to hear sounds as though the structure was giving up its fight to stand. I had one more chance.

I slammed my body against the door, piercing my arms through the barred window and bear-hugging them on the opposite side. I railed furiously against the stubborn might of the door, and the palace guard to my side yelled in anger as he levered his weight against his pry bar. The door gave, but it was too late.

With a groaning crash like the howl of the underworld itself, the building above relented to the flames. Tons of burning wood, steel, and stone came crashing down like an avalanche. For a moment that seemed frozen in time, our eyes met through the bars on the door held tightly in my arms. Her eyes said more at that moment than words could in a lifetime. Fire, sparks, and smoke danced all around her, and the crashing sound was deafening. I saw nothing else;

and heard nothing else. There was nothing but her eyes.

You tried. They said.

For the second time that day, I plunged into that dark abyss of emotional numbness. The waves overtook me. The dark ocean swallowed me up once more. I knew the guard was dragging me towards the exit, but this time there was a new sensation. Somehow, I realized; just as darkness took me deep within its shadow; I could not feel my arms.

# THE LAST POST

Linda smiled as she watched a hummingbird through her kitchen window. It danced around the feeder that hung from a post attached to the deck, darting in to drink the nectar and then away before coming back again, never resting on the feeder's perch. At one point, a second bird joined the feast, before eventually the pair chased one another off. Linda finished washing a sterile white coffee mug and dipped it in rinse water before placing it on a drying rack beside the sink. She took a short stack of dirty plates and dipped them into the dishwater, retrieving the top plate and beginning to wash it as she ran through a mental checklist for the day.

*Closed the Finderman deal this morning, have to remember to arrange to pick up the keys with the client. Should call Elliot after dinner. Glad James is on dinner duty tonight… kids are home in two hours, new client interview is in 45 minutes. Should be able to get these dishes done in plenty of time. What was their name again?*

Linda dipped the plate into the rinse water and set it on the drying rack. She dried her hands on a towel lying on her counter near the rack and reached into her back pocket to retrieve her phone. A quick hold of her thumb over the print scanner and the smartphone screen flashed to life. A lovely picture of her family laughing at the side of the lake was partially obscured by an arranged assortment of application icons. She tapped one of the icons, a picture of a house with a golden star inside it. The application came to life, with information on real estate listings, a calendar, and an e-mail inbox all built into one. She clicked the calendar.

*Right. Niels family. LGBTQ2+ couple. Two adopted children. Looking for a quaint home in a family neighbourhood.*

Linda clicked the listings section of the application, making a mental note of listed homes she could propose to the buyers. A notification chimed up on her phone from one of her social media applications. The local radio station running a "Caption this!" contest for tickets to the upcoming

Rock on the Riverside festival. Linda hesitated for a moment, and then tapped the notification, her phone switching over to the new application almost instantly. The picture was a young teen boy in mid-air during a bicycle jump, and his shocked expression as he realizes he is about to collide with the parked car he had been trying to jump. Linda chuckled as she concentrated on the boy's expression; his furrowed brow, squinting eyes, and gritted teeth.

*Bet I know what's going through his head right now.*

Linda scrolled through the captions others had already posted. Most were mundane, or not at all funny. Some referenced insurance company slogans. Some questioned the whereabouts of the boy's parents. Two comments were offensive, which always made Linda cringe. Hundreds of people had already posted angry reactions to the offensive comments. Linda ignored them. She knew better than to get involved with social media disputes.

Deciding she had nothing witty to say, Linda instead switched her phone to the camera application and took a picture through the kitchen window of the now-returned hummingbird at the feeder. She opened her social media page and started a post with the picture, tagging her real estate brand and captioning the photo with the hashtags: #homeownerlife and #trulyblessed. Then she returned her phone to her back pocket and continued washing the dishes. She had just rinsed and placed the last plate on the rack when there was a loud knock at the door. A muffled voice shouted something incoherent from the other side.

Linda dried her hands as she crossed her kitchen and rounded the corner of her living room toward the front door. The knocking continued, louder and more forceful this time. The voice on the other side was male and sounded like law enforcement.

"Linda Bailey. This is Agent Armand from Social Response. Open up!"

Linda felt her breath catch in her throat as she heard the man's words. Her hands shook as she opened the door. She was greeted by three men and a woman, all wearing charcoal suits and shined shoes. The man who had been knocking slowly lowered his hand. He had a dark complexion and even darker hair, but his eyes were sky blue.

"Linda Bailey?" Agent Armand said as he pulled a smartphone from the inside pocket of his jacket. Linda nodded, words escaping her. "May we come in?"

Linda stepped aside and the agents rushed in at the implied invitation. The female agent was carrying a duffel bag as she rushed passed Linda along with the other male agent who was standing with her in the back. The pair bolted up the stairs toward the bedrooms. Agent Armand and the remaining agent stepped calmly into the entranceway and closed the front door.

"What is this?" Linda breathed, "What is going on?"

Agent Armand held up his phone. On the screen was a picture of Linda from her early 20s shortly before she obtained her Real Estate license. The picture was from a trip she and some friends had taken to Africa. She and her friends were intoxicated. They were posing in front of a taxidermy elephant. The caption on the photo read "Drunk as fuuuuuuck in Africa!! Check out this elephant my Uncle shot, yo!! The beast is huuuuuuuung!!"

"Do you recognize this post?" Agent Armand said. He continued when Linda nodded, clearly shocked and ashamed.

"Does the name Nick Bolas mean anything to you?"

Linda nodded. "He's a competitor. Another real estate agent."

Agent Armand flicked his phone, tapping through various posts on the same social media application Linda belonged to. Upstairs, the two agents were rummaging through closets and dressers and not at all being quiet about it. The fourth agent, a tall blonde man, was looking through the blinds out into the driveway as though waiting for something to happen. Linda couldn't help but notice the service pistol attached to his hip. Agent Armand finally held up his phone, causing Linda to gasp and cover her mouth with her hands.

On the agent's phone, Linda saw the post from Africa, shared by Nick Bolas with the caption: "Your trusted local real estate agent? More like a toxic spoiled MURDERER! Do you really want to trust your future to this? She is EVIL! #burnLindaBailey." Already, there were over two hundred comments, some claiming to have heard first-hand accounts of Linda's love of hunting. Some called for her to be run out of town. Others called for violence. Even so-called 'friends' were starting to post pictures of her out of context, showing Linda in the outdoors wearing hiking gear that the poster claimed was for 'sport hunting.' Linda's phone chimed in her back pocket. Shaking, she took it out. It was a text message from the Niels couple.

Just saw your picture, Linda. The text began. We can't believe we were going to work with you! God… this is 2028… we have no interest in being associated with someone like you. You disgust us!

"This…" Linda whimpered, her hands shaking as she tried unsuccessfully to type a reply. "This can't be happening… I don't even hunt… I'm not…"

Agent Armand sympathetically reached out and lowered Linda's phone, taking it away from her and passing it to the blonde agent at the door.

"We know, Linda. That's why we're here. The Social Response Agency protects people like you. Unfortunate victims of social smear campaigns. We mobilized as soon as we saw the burn Linda Bailey hashtag go viral. The agents upstairs are gathering your things as we speak. We have to get you out of here. The Agency predicts a flash mob within the next few hours given your position and notoriety within your career and this community."

"A… flash mob?"

The blonde agent answered a phone call, his eyes still fixed on the driveway and the cul-de-sac beyond. Agent Armand began leading Linda toward the door.

"Your life as you know it is over, Linda. This type of campaign will be harsh and unyielding. You will be moved, and given a new identity."

"This is crazy… what about my family? Where is my family?"

"They are safe," Agent Armand said, at the moment the two agents upstairs began descending with full duffel bags in tow. "A team has already picked up your husband from work and is in transit to the safe house. A second team is picking up your children from school."

"Sir," the blonde agent interrupted, "Charlie team has the children, but there's been an incident. It appears the campaign reached some of the children at school and the youngest has suffered injuries."

"Injuries?" Linda demanded, suddenly angry as well as afraid. "What kind of injuries? What happened to my daughter?"

The blonde agent shook his head and opened the door, allowing the two agents with the bags to exit the house. "Minor injuries. She's alright. Medical aid is already on the way to the safe house. It looks like she was jumped by some kids at school."

Agent Armand motioned Linda out and nodded at the Blonde agent, who returned to the phone call as he also exited the house, closing the front door behind him.

"Jumped by kids at school? This can't be happening… she didn't do anything!"

Agent Armand led Linda toward an unmarked black SUV parked in their driveway. Linda's phone rang, and the blonde agent looked at it.

"Who is that?" Linda demanded as they neared the SUV. Having finished loading the bags, the female agent opened the passenger-side rear door for Linda to get in.

"It's your office. No doubt you've just been fired. The campaign is moving fast. We need to get you out of here."

After Linda climbed into the SUV, the female agent closed the door and climbed into the passenger seat in the front. She opened the glove box and pulled out what looked like a pistol with a round drum attached to the barrel. Agent Armand climbed into the driver's seat, while the blonde and remaining agents climbed into a small black sedan. The SUV screeched onto the road, and the car pulled out of the driveway behind them.

Linda looked out her window back toward her house. It looked so serene, so normal. The sprinkler was still going on the front lawn, watering the garden she had planted with her daughter last spring. Her roses and lilies were in bloom. The comprehension of everything that was happening seemed so far away. She thought of the dishes still drying on the rack inside. She thought of the hummingbirds she had taken a photo of not yet an hour ago. Her teeth gritted, and her knuckles turned white from gripping the door. As the SUV rolled down the street, she turned her eyes away from her home.

Ahead of them, some of her neighbours had started coming out of their houses into the street. Most of them she had recognized from Halloweens trick or treating with her kids, or summer block parties. Now, they swarmed from their homes like ants, cell phones raised like drooling mandibles, ready to tear down one of those among them over false allegations blasted across cyberspace. One of the neighbours, a woman named Cindy, raised her phone to take a picture of the SUV as it sped by. The female agent acted quickly.

The strange pistol made a thumping whir sound as the agent pulled the trigger, aimed directly at Cindy. Almost instantly, Cindy's phone sparked and she jumped, dropping the smoking unit to the ground. Amazingly, the passenger window that was rolled up the whole time was not affected. The pistol echoed its strange sound over and over as more people attempted to photograph the fleeing car. Linda watched as all their phones were fried, falling to the ground one after another every time the pistol fired. Finally, the SUV rounded a bend onto the main road and the female agent relaxed into her seat. Agent Armand made eye contact with Linda in his rearview mirror.

"Are you alright?"

The question hit Linda in the pit of her stomach like a hammer driving a railway spike. Tears rolled down her face and her whole body shook.

"I was 21!" she screamed. "21! And I was drunk!! That was my Uncle's trophy! What the hell is wrong with this world?"

The female agent stored the strange pistol back in the glove box as Agent Armand turned his eyes back to the road. He swung the SUV onto an on-ramp for the freeway.

"Unfortunately for some, Mrs. Bailey, the new social world we live in allows for one mistake, sometimes even none at all. Everything is recorded. Nothing is forgotten. We've seen the good you put in the world, otherwise, we wouldn't be here. But the new world is a witch-hunt. Even innocent, once accused, all we can do is help you disappear."

"But why me? Why is this happening?"

"You had a weakness in your past, Mrs. Bailey. You made enemies in your profession. Competition. It was only a matter of time."

"So… if you had the power to find me, to help me, why not just get rid of that picture in the first place?"

"For the same reason you couldn't get rid of it, Mrs. Bailey. We are a reactive agency, and there's no way to know what's out there for everyone, or whether they truly are people worth saving. When we saw Nick's post and saw the campaign ignite, we did our homework on you and your family. You have the resources and the capability to start again."

"And what does the agency get out of helping me?"

There was a long silence. "Half."

Linda gulped, fearing she already knew the answer to her question. "Half what?"

Agent Armand signalled a lane change, taking the freeway route out of town toward the industrial district and the airport.

"Half of everything. All your assets will be liquidated. Your identities resolved. You'll get a fresh start, and half your assets to set you up in your new lives."

"How often does this happen."

Agent Armand met Linda's eyes through the rearview mirror. His jaw was set, and his expression looked hollow. His shining blue eyes appeared empty.

"Too often."

For the next forty minutes or so, the SUV barreled along the freeway, eventually taking the exit that led to the international airport outside of town. Linda alternated from crying and shaking, to anger and resentment. She was exhausted, driven only by adrenaline, and in shock. The memory of that night, twenty years ago in Africa, played through her mind over and over again like a movie. It wracked her with guilt. She wished she could throttle the younger version of herself for ever posting it. But then, who could have predicted this would be the outcome? How could anyone have imagined a world where a single social media post could derail the lives of an entire family?

"We're here."

Agent Armand's voice broke Linda out of her daze and she looked up to find they were approaching a hangar on the backside of the airport. A plane was on the tarmac, its cabin door open. Three other vehicles were parked outside the hangar. It was then that Linda noticed the sedan that had been at her home was no longer with them. As they came to a stop near the other cars, a familiar face popped out of the open cabin of the plane. Linda's tears flowed freely and she sobbed, throwing open the SUV door and running toward the plane as a tall bearded man ran down the stairs to greet her.

"Mike!" she screamed as she fell shaking into his arms. "Mike I'm so sorry…"

"It's okay," Mike said, stroking her hair. "It's okay. That's not who you are. We know."

By this time, Linda's son and daughter had exited the plane to greet their mother. Linda dropped to her knees and held her daughter's face in her hands. Her left eye was bruised and swollen, and a bandage covered her forehead above the eye. A wad of gauze plugging her left nostril was crimson with blood. Linda sobbed so much she could barely form words.

"I'm so… so sorry this happened to you…"

Linda's daughter shrugged.

"It's okay, Mommy. I told them they were assholes."

"Linda," Mike said as he pulled her to her feet. "The agents got to her before it got worse. The teachers let it happen, Linda…"

"What?"

Agent Armand and the female agent passed the family on the way to the plane. They carried the duffel bags packed at the house up the stairs and into the cabin.

"It's scary, Linda. It's like the whole world has written us off… look at this…"

Mike pulled his work cell out of his pocket, checking around for agents first. He tapped the screen a couple of times and held a photo out to show Linda.

"Diego texted it to me. Remember him? He sat with us at the Christmas party last year. He and his wife Rolanda. Anyways… that's our house, Linda. Not even half an hour ago. Look what those bastards did to it…"

Linda's hands shook as she took the phone from Mike. The lawn was gouged up, as though someone had ripped it up with a dirt bike. The garden flowers were chopped down and trampled. Windows were broken, and the word 'murderer' was spray-painted across the garage door along with many other damning phrases.

"This can't be real…" she squeaked, her voice

barely a broken whisper.

"You shouldn't look at things like that," Agent Armand said, surprising Mike, who reluctantly took his phone back from Linda and surrendered it to the agent. "Believe me, Mr. Bailey. It's best if you cut all ties with your previous life now. Campaigns like this don't go away. All you can do now is start over, and keep clean on everything."

Agent Armand held his hand out gesturing to the plane. The Bailey family nodded silently and began making their way toward the stairs. Linda stopped and turned to Agent Armand.

"Where are we going?" she asked.

"I'm not allowed to know, Mrs. Bailey. For your own safety. A new team will meet you at your destination. The pilot has been briefed. They will give you your new identities and assist you with settling in."

The female agent approached and handed Agent Armand a data pad.

"When?" he asked her.

"Thirteen minutes ago."

Agent Armand nodded and handed the datapad back to the female agent. "Dispatch the teams. We're on our way."

As the female agent turned and headed for the SUV, Agent Armand turned his attention back to the Bailey family.

"Duty calls," he began. "Safe travels Bailey family. Good luck."

Linda nodded. "Agent Armand?" she called as he began to walk away. He stopped and looked over his shoulder.

"Thank you."

Agent Armand smiled and walked away, as Mike guided Linda toward the plane and up the stairs. As she was seated in her chair beside Mike and the children, Linda looked out the window onto the tarmac. She watched the black SUV and two sedans as they raced out of the airport and disappeared into the traffic in the distance. Suddenly she was reminded of the hummingbirds. She smiled, despite everything.

"What's the smile for?" Mike asked, leaning over her to look out at the tarmac.

"Hummingbird," she replied. "This morning, I was watching a hummingbird at our feeder. Another one came and they fought and chased each other off. But eventually… the first one came back to the feeder, so I posted a picture of it."

"I don't get it…" Mike said, sitting back in his chair confused.

Linda smiled and sat back in her chair. She looked at her kids, her son helping his sister put her seatbelt on, and she looked at Mike. She wiped the last of her tears from her eyes and thought about her family's future. What they would do with their fresh start. She patted Mike's forearm.

"You don't need to."

# PACO

I blink two or three times as my eyes open. The light coming in my window is dim… but it hurts anyway. I want to close my eyes again; and sink back into the nothingness of dreams. I find no comfort though. Closing my eyes only breeds chaos in my mind.

Sweat-soaked sheets slide to the floor as I swing my legs from the bed. Cold sweat. Fever again. The dim light from the neon sign outside is flickering. The sound against the glass tells me why. It's raining again. I feel like I want to yawn, but my mouth doesn't seem to want to do what I tell it to. There's a stiffness in my neck as I turn to look at the pillow. I long for sleep. Nothing finds me in the darkness of my mind that I can control. Nothing I can forget.

I drop my head into my hands. Cold steel meets

my face. A stoic reminder of everything in my life I have come to hate. A solemn reminder of the worst decision I have ever made. Synapses fire and the world fades. I hate this part. It makes me feel sick.

There is bright light. It hurts my eyes… like looking into a white-hot sun. The doctors tell me I won't feel a thing. Phantoms hiding their demonic cackles behind paper masks. I feel it though. I feel every second of it. The scream tears the flashback to pieces and catapults me back through my mangled past.

I hear gunfire. I smell cordite and burning flesh. Arid heat from the desert sun burns my skin, somehow piercing through the layers of combat clothing and load-bearing rigs. Sweat stings my eyes, running freely from the spongy headband I wear under my Kevlar helmet. At least the light isn't so bad. The searing sun is shaded by the ballistic lenses barely holding on to my sweat-soaked face. Dust crunches under my boots. At least I hope it's dust.

I hear a whizzing sound, and the man beside me falls to the ground gasping for air through a severed esophagus. I drop to a knee, returning fire with one hand as I drag the boy behind the cover. He is frantically grasping his throat. I can't help myself but stare at his tongue as it whips about in a frenzy. He fights me as I attempt to move his hands and see the wound. I can see why. The gash across his neck has cut his jugular and his windpipe. There's nothing I can do. After a moment, his thrashing stops. His eyes glaze, and I notice that the blood running from his wound is a trickle. His name was Burlanson. My hand shakes as I hold it up. My gloves are red with his blood. There is a hard impact on the air; A sound like dropping a rock underwater. Everything goes black.

I'm in my room again. The sweat running from my chest feels like ice. My arm is even colder. They told me it would be a smooth transition. Teaches me to sign contracts I don't understand. "Soldier recovery bionics" they called it. Research program. A fancy name for a guinea pig. The grenade that had hit me tore my right arm off halfway down the bicep. I run my real hand through the lifeless steel palm and up the wrist. Where the metal meets the skin, I wince. My body is rejecting the arm. I need my drugs.

The bathroom is filthy. It smells of rot and vomit. The nurse will be here tomorrow, she can clean it up. She's a royal bitch anyways. I take the glass cup off the counter. It's so hard to resist using the metal arm; I was right-handed before. I don't like the feeling of things when I use it; nothing feels like it should. Inside the medicine cabinet, I find the drugs the doctors gave me. Supposedly they help the circuitry interface with my nervous system. I don't understand any of it, but if it makes the pain go away, then I'll take them. I hate them though, almost as much as I hate this arm. They make my head spin. I take them anyway.

"This is going to take time for you to adapt," they said. I can hear their voices in my head as the room starts to swim. "Due to the nature of the arms link to your nervous system, there may be some complications."

Complications. That's what they called it. Constant pain, infections, fever. Not to mention the alien feeling I get every time I touch anything with this thing. Without knowing it, I ball my fist. The bionics tear a basketball-sized hole in the wall like the cement is made of Styrofoam. I don't feel a thing. There's a bit of a whine as my head clears and I pull my arm out of the hole. Good. I hope I broke something. I asked them before to take this thing out of me. Let me be natural. They said they can't. They want to study the effects. So they locked me up in this concrete dungeon and sent nurses and doctors in four times a day to study how my body is reacting to the machinery.

I'm starting to go crazy. Maybe it's the drugs. Maybe it's the constant pain. Maybe it's the betrayal. I don't know how much more of this I can take. I hold the hand up in front of my face. The fingers are disproportionately large. It's heavy, but the pins and exoskeletal supports in my legs and spine hold the weight. They hurt too.

The cement dust from punching the wall coats the palm and the fingers. I can see abrasions and dents. Suddenly, looking at the hand, an idea hits me that I never thought of before. With surprising finality, I realize I've found my way out.

The hand holds my face like I'm palming a basketball. The steel is cold against my burning skin and sweat. I send the command, and my world turns black, one last time.

# EMERGENCE

The whiskey burned his throat as Erik took a long drink straight from the bottle. He coughed, running his hand through his curly brown hair as he passed the bottle to his right. The man who took it slapped his rotund belly, making everyone around the campfire laugh.

"Get in ma belly!" the large man said, silencing himself with the bottle and tilting it almost vertically.

"Come on man," said a third man, his thinning hairline indicating early onset of pattern baldness. "Hog it all and I'll piss in your tent!"

A large campfire shed dancing orange light across the four men as they laughed and spread the warmth of the whiskey among one another. Occasionally, the flames tossed tiny embers skyward, which were quickly whipped away by the wind. Not even the smoke was rising straight up from the fire, instead leaning to and fro like the inflatable tube men one might find at a car dealership.

The wind was symptomatic of the storm that was brewing, completely ignored by the inebriated men surrounding the fire. Out on the lake they camped beside, waves licked skyward, their whitecaps driven by the wind. Lightning strikes lit up the sky, and thunder rolled around the valley that cradled the lake. One particular lightning strike hit a tree on the mountainside, sending shards of broken wood across the forest. With the wind blowing as it was, it did not take long for the shattered tree to glow with the beginnings of its own fire.

Back at the camp, only a mile or so away, the men drank and partied. They were completely unaware of the danger they were in, not even hearing the thunder over the sound of their blaring music and their laughter. The storm carried no rain, and this late in the summer, the forest was a tinder box. Unfortunately, Mother Nature had lit the match.

"Where you going, Walrus?" Erik asked as the large man stood and staggered uneasily on his feet.

"It's Russ, jackass. And I'm goin for a leak. Want to come hold it for me?"

Erik and the other two men laughed. The balding man passed the whiskey across the fire to the fourth man, a burly red-haired lad with a bushy beard. As he did, he nodded toward Russ as the big man lumbered off into the dark woods.

"Better go with him, Erik. He'll need someone to help him find it under that belly."

"I heard that, Lindon… tough talk. I got more hair on my balls than you do on your head!" Russ called back as he started to fade into the dark beyond the campfire light.

Lindon picked up a rock and tossed it in Russ' general direction, general being a generous term. The rock sailed into the dark nowhere near Russ. The red-haired man took a sip of whiskey and handed the bottle back to Erik. He leaned forward and sprayed a breath of liquor into the fire, causing a small fireball to erupt.

"I'm a damn ginger dragon!" he roared.

"Jesus Kurt! Waste of whiskey, man…" Lindon said.

"Don't be a bitch. You're just mad you never thought of it." Kurt barked back.

Lindon leaned back in his camp chair, digging deep into his pocket and producing a thick-rolled joint.

"Why breathe fire when breathing smoke is so much better?"

Erik and Kurt nodded their approval, and a round of cheers went up, echoing across the lake. Lindon pulled a stick from the fire and used the burning end to light his joint, taking a pair of deep puffs off it and passing it to Kurt while at the same time returning the stick to the fire. He held his breath in for a moment while Kurt took a big drag and passed the joint on.

When at last Lindon released his lung full of smoke, he leaned back in his chair, feigning passing out.

Erik took the joint from Kurt just as Russ came back from the edge of the darkness. He was drawing up the zipper in his pants. He stopped at a large black truck with a canopy on it that was parked off the edge of their campsite. A cooler inside the canopy revealed a heaping pile of beer and other alcohol, along with hotdogs and other simple camp food. He pulled a six-pack of beer from the cooler and returned to the fire. Erik was holding out the joint for him when he reached his chair.

"Fuck that," Russ said, waving the offer away. "Got all a man needs right here, boys."

With that, Russ plunged his girth into his chair and cracked open one of the beers. The joint made its way back to Lindon while the others chided their companion.

"You'd be half your size if you did this shit instead of that shit…" Lindon pointed out. Russ flipped him the middle finger in response as he chugged his beer down. In an instant, he finished the can, crushed it, and tossed the empty aside all while opening a new one with his other hand.

"God your redneck energy is impressive sometimes," Kurt began, rubbing his hands over his chest and pretending to stroke his nipples. "Makes me horny."

"Oh dear God…" Erik said through fits of laughter.

The night wore on in much the same fashion, as alcohol and marijuana flowed freely amongst the group. Stories of high school glory days, sexual conquests, fights, and workplace drama were intertwined with belch competitions and more than one drinking race which Russ won every single time. The storm never released a single drop of rain, and so the boys continued their obliviousness to it. The winds had picked up ever so slightly, fanning the flames of the wildfire brewing in the forest. It had grown steadily in the hours since the lightning struck, and now almost the entirety of the hill on the Southern side of the lake was on fire. Embers tossed by the wind from the burning trees seeded new fire, and every so slowly the blaze grew closer to the campsite.

Russ stood from his chair, only one single remaining beer in the pack he had grabbed earlier hung from the plastic rings. The other men chided his tiny bladder as he stumbled away from the fire again, heading for the edge of darkness where he could relieve himself. As he passed the truck, he set the beer down on the tailgate. Beyond the trucks, the road into the campsite turned a bit to the right and gradually rose to meet the main forestry road that came into the lake. It was here, in the ditch at the edge of the road, that Russ had decided earlier was far enough away from the camp to do his business.

As before, he lowered his zipper and bounced his penis free of pants. In a moment, he was relieving himself in a healthy stream off into the forest. Dramatically, he threw his head back and ushered the loudest ah sound that he could, hoping the guys would notice. Of course, they didn't. They were too busy listening to some story Kurt was telling about a new human resources lady they had at work. Russ shook his head and looked out into the dark woods ahead of him. His night vision was just beginning to recover from the light of the fire, and the trees were an eerie portal into the night. They looked foggy, almost glowing with a strange ambient light. Russ thought he saw shapes racing by in the darkness.

Still urinating, Russ grunted and leaned forward, squinting his eyes to see into the trees. Just then, something lunged out of the woods directly at him. He squeaked and fell over backwards, his stream splashing all over his belly and his pants as two more shapes like the first darted past, and then a fourth. Russ rolled over onto his belly and watched the deer bolt across the road and vanish into the dark forest on the other side.

"What the actual…"

Before he could finish his sentence, a huge buck stepped out of the dark woods and stopped almost on top of him. Even in the dark, the impressive rack of horns on the buck's head caught Russ' attention. He counted at least five points per side in the horns of the creature, still covered with summer velvet. The buck looked down at Russ lying on the dirt road, then back the way it had come in the forest. Suddenly, it let out a shrill cry unlike anything Russ had heard in his life, before darting off across the road into the woods.

Russ shook with shock. He climbed to his feet, completely forgetting about his piss-soaked clothes or his penis which wagged to and fro as he ran like a tiny hairless tail. As fast as his girth and intoxication would allow, he plunged toward the campfire and the safety of his friends.

When Russ finally fell into the firelight, having tripped over a root just behind his chair, the others leapt to their feet. At first, they were surprised, but when Russ stood and they saw his manhood hanging out and the front of his pants soaking wet, they exploded with laughter. Russ was desperate to catch his breath and waved his hands in the air frantically.

"I told you he needed help holding it!" Lindon was saying through tears.

"Oh mama, come to your ginger daddy!" Kurt exclaimed.

"Fu..." Russ gasped.

"Holy shit, Russ... did you piss all over yourself?" Erik was asking, looking at the wet stains on Russ' pants. "He pissed all over himself!! Oh God... it smells like asparagus..."

"Fu..." still Russ couldn't speak.

"Fuh, fuh, fuh..." Lindon mocked before Kurt finished the sentence for him. "Fuckin samsquantch!!"

As the boys laughed, Russ drew a deep breath and bent over. Finally, he roared out what he was trying to say.

"Fucking MONSTER buck!"

Immediately the boys silenced. They looked at Russ in surprise. Russ held up his hand, fingers splayed open to show all five including his thumb.

"Five points. Came out of the woods like the devil. Knocked me on my ass."

Erik stood up.

"Shut up."

Russ was shaking his head.

"No bullshit," he said. "Five points. Came outta the woods at mach nine, at least four does with him."

"Where did they go?" Kurt asked.

Erik pointed off to the South side of the campsite, roughly in the direction the deer had gone.

"Some…" Russ fought to catch his breath. "Something spooked them, guys. Buck screamed like nothing I ever heard before."

"No way, Russ…" Lindon was saying, swaying on his chair. "You're messing with us. That sound was you, man. That wasn't no buck."

"Yeah man," Erik said. "We heard you scream *run* like a little girl."

Russ looked shocked.

"I never said a word. Swear it. The buck stopped almost right on top of me, screamed back into the woods, then ran off. Pissed on myself sure, but that sound near made me shit too."

Erik, Kurt, and Lindon looked at one another in turn, while Russ took the opportunity to finally tuck his penis away.

"So hold up…" Lindon said, standing to his feet but swaying as he did so. "You're saying… and we *all* heard it… that a five-point buck screamed *run* and then ran off into the night?"

Russ shook his head in disgust and then looked around for the last beer he had had earlier.

"Damn it you guys, the buck didn't say *run*. Just screamed this horrid sound off into the woods and then bolted. You smoked too much of that shit if you think it said *run*."

"What would it want us to run from, you guys?" Erik asked.

"Jesus man… I have no idea…" Kurt replied.

"Bears maybe?" added Lindon.

Russ turned and walked back toward the tailgate of his truck, suddenly dubious of the darkness beyond the firelight. He shivered, his wet pants finally making him notice the wind. As he reached the end of the pickup, Russ realized the fog he saw earlier was thicker now and was moving across their campsite in the direction the deer had run. Squinting in the dark, he noticed the fog had an odd behaviour to it. He sniffed the air. Not fog, smoke.

Russ turned and looked at their campfire. The fingers of flame that licked upwards were tipped near horizontal by a crosswind that the men hadn't noticed all night while they were drinking. Thick smoke blew through the campsite, none of it from their fire. Russ made his way to the cab of the truck and opened the door. He shut off the radio, to the surprise of his companions.

"Russ man, what…"

Russ cut Erik off with a raised hand. In the silence that finally followed, the group heard a faint and far-off crackling sound. Slowly, Russ backed away from the truck and turned his attention skyward. The clouds to the North that dotted the sky told the guys the trouble they were in. A faint orange and red glow tinted the gray-black clouds against the night sky.

"Holy shit guys" Russ swallowed hard. "I think that's a wildfire."

"What are we gonna do?" asked Lindon, stepping around his chair to get a better look at the sky.

"We gotta get out of here, guys. Now!" Said Kurt.

Russ' head hurt. Not just from fear, but because he was so drunk, he could barely focus.

"None of us can drive…" he stuttered.

"Fuck that!" shouted Kurt. "We can't stay here man… you heard that deer! We gotta run, man."

Erik and Lindon, spurred into action by Kurt's panic, started to sprint for the truck but only ended up tripping over their chairs and the other camp implements strewn about the site. In short order, the whole group had descended into chaos, and Russ panicked. Despite his brain fog, Russ knew that trying to drive out of the bush in their state, even with the threat of a wildfire barreling down on them, was tantamount to suicide. Reacting on instinct, he reached back into the truck and removed the keys, hurling them over the heads of his companions and out into the woods. The guys froze and stared at Russ.

"What…" Kurt said, climbing to his feet. "What did you just do?"

Russ was in shock. His head was spinning.

"Russ, what the fuck? You just killed us, man."

Erik and Kurt looked at Lindon after his words rolled out of his mouth.

"Yeah…" Erik agreed, nodding his head and standing slowly. "Yeah, you just killed us, Russ!"

"Russ' buck said to run, man… how are we gonna run now, Russ?"

All three guys were on their feet now, moving toward Russ, who began heaving as though he was about to throw up. Erik, Kurt, and Lindon pounced on Russ, knocking him to the ground. They shouted and pulled at Russ, trying to drag him toward the campfire. They punched and kicked at him, yelling obscenities and threats. Russ rolled on the ground, shielding his face with his arms and not fighting back. He pleaded that he was sorry, over and again. Paranoia and intoxication ruled the mob, so they pressed their attack. Then Kurt let out a strange grunt.

Erik stopped his attack on Russ, while Lindon continued. Erik looked at Kurt, whose eyes had gone wide. His red beard and curly hair shone in the firelight. Before Erik could ask what had happened, Kurt grunted again, this time more like a cough, and warm fluid splashed Erik's face. Kurt suddenly slid away from the group as though pulled by a great force. Lindon's attack stopped then, and Russ finally lowered the guard on his face.

Kurt lay prone on the dirt of the campsite a few feet from the dogpile the guys were in. He was close to the tail end of the truck, where the canopy was still open. The cooler that had been in the back of the truck was smashed to pieces on the ground. Firelight illuminated a hulking mass of charred flesh and burnt hair, terrible muscle, claws, and teeth. The form stood over and on top of Kurt's back, powerful jaws sunk into the lower part of his back above his hips. A huge paw tipped with claws like rock pikes pressed down on Kurt between his shoulder blades.

Kurt spat and tried to call for help, but as soon as he budged at all, the Grizzly bit harder into his spine and pressed down with his paws. Kurt's eyes blinked, and his ginger head sunk into the dirt. Russ, Erik, and Lindon could almost see the life leave his eyes by the firelight. Sensing that his prey was dead, the grizzly turned his attention to the rest of the group. It took a step toward them, revealing more of itself in the campfire light.

The bear had been burned horribly. Half of its face had been scorched away almost to bone in some places along its cheek. The ear on the burnt side of its face was seared away also, and there was a mess of scorched and blistered hair and skin down the shoulder and back. The creature took a menacing step toward the group, Kurt's blood dripping from its jaws. The boys were locked in terror. The bear was like a demon from their darkest nightmares stalking toward them.

Just then, the forest behind them erupted with light as a flaming tree crashed through the woods near their camp. Sparks and flames shot across the road, born on the wind, setting tiny new fires all around them. The bear panicked and ran off into the woods, fleeing the hellfire that had scarred it.

The guys had no time to process what had just happened. The wildfire had saved them from the bear, but now they found themselves quite literally out of the frying pan, and into the fire. The roar of the forest burning was an assault on their ears. The paint on the truck was starting to boil and melt away, as was the fibreglass of the canopy. Russ was first to scramble to his feet, and without thinking, he grabbed Erik's shirt and started dragging him towards the edge of the lake.

It took a moment for Lindon to understand Russ' intention through his drug and alcohol-induced stupor, but he eventually started to follow. He was about twenty feet or so behind his friends when Russ reached their aluminum fishing boat and practically threw Erik in. Lindon was charging towards them as fast as he could go. He watched Russ turn and beckon to him.

"Run!" Russ was screaming. "Run you idiot!"

Lindon never made it to the boat. Just as he was about to clear the edge of the forest onto the small beach where the boat was, a flaming tree came down in his path, knocking him to the ground. The last Erik and Russ saw of him was his hand trying in vain to wave off the sweltering heat of the fire. Knowing there was nothing more he could do; Russ shoved the boat off into the safety of the lake and dove in.

As he paddled them closer to the middle of the lake, Russ had his first good look at the devastation of the fire. Almost all the mountainside was engulfed in flame now, spurred on impossibly fast by the winds. Thick smoke rolled skyward, blocking out the stars and clouds in the night sky. Everything, even the shining water of the lake, was awash in a reddish-orange hue. A pop erupted in the woods, and a small mushroom cloud of fire rose above the trees. The truck's gas tank, no doubt.

The thought of the truck made Russ think of Kurt and Lindon. He hurled over the edge of the boat into the lake. Erik had long since thrown up on himself and passed out from shock. He was crumbled in the front of the boat, breathing shallow. Russ watched the fire for a time, scooped up some of the lake water for a drink, threw up again, and then finally curled into the bottom of the boat himself to sleep. Blessed sleep took him, and as the world around them burned violently, they drifted safely amid the still waters of the lake.

********

Russel Eradin Plansky and Erik Scott Alden were recovered safely by Wildfire Services after their

175

campsite was caught in the path of the Kindle Lake wildfire in 2023. The two men were found drifting together in the lake in a twelve-foot aluminum rowboat. Two of their companions, Kurtis Albrecht Cameron and Lindon Michael Elroy lost their lives in the blaze when they were unable to reach the safety of the boat with the others. The wildfire, caused by lightning, destroyed over 100,000 hectares of forest and thirty-seven structures in two communities. It only claimed the lives of two people.

# THE HAUNTING OF OLD MAN RITTER

Franklin Aloysius Ritter passed away in his own home on the 18th of April 2021. Autopsy reports released to the public after his death cited the cause as "acute respiratory failure due to COVID-19 infection and related complications." He was 94 years old.

Old Man Ritter, as he was known to the community, was an isolated hermit with no known living relatives or surviving family. He lived on a small acreage fourteen kilometres outside the town of Brightwood, British Columbia. His small cottage-style home was the sole building at the end of an unnamed road. Locals referred to it as Ritter Road.

Upon his death, a small service was held in the

town's senior citizen center, but only three people attended. I was one of them, attending on behalf of the local paper as a journalist. I found it sad that a man had lived such a long life in a small community, yet collected no friends to attend his funeral. As I perused the small collection of his belongings that had been put on display, I made small talk with the president of the seniors center, one of the other guests.

The story of Old Man Ritter began to captivate me as the president recounted local legends of the hermit. There was no reason for his exile from society that anyone could see. He was nice enough in all his interactions when he did come to town. He never smiled though, and never spoke a single word more than he needed to, which led me to believe his isolation was self-imposed. Some people thought he was nefarious, others pitied him, but all kept their distance for whatever reason.

As far as anyone could tell, Old Man Ritter had always lived in the cottage at the end of Ritter Road. The president had grown up in the town of Brightwood, eventually retiring and running the senior citizen's center on behalf of the residents. They had a large membership and ran all sorts of events for social gatherings. Not surprisingly, Ritter never attended a single one despite constant invitations. The president was one of the few locals curious about the strange hermit, and it had been her who had arranged the funeral for him.

The only other guest aside from myself and the president was a local constable. He had been the one to respond to a request for a wellness check on Old Man Ritter. The call had come from the local pharmacist, who was alerted when Ritter failed to pick up his prescription drugs on time. This was incredibly out of character, and so the alarm had been raised.

The constable was a conversational man and had chosen to make the appearance at the funeral out of respect. He was off duty for the event and spoke freely when I asked for details of his response. For the most part, there were no details about the wellness check that were outside the ordinary. The constable had arrived, knocked, had no answer, and looked through a window to discover Old Man Ritter lying unconscious on the floor. With grounds for entry, he made the radio calls and entered the home to find Ritter dead on arrival. There was no evidence at all of foul play, and no investigation followed. But a hesitation in the constable's voice indicated there was more to the story, and my journalistic instinct drove me onward.

Unable to explain it in words, the constable simply indicated a feeling of intense unease in the home while he waited for paramedics and the coroner to arrive. He was alone in the home, yet heard strange noises and a few times, saw movement out of the corner of his eyes. A skeptic, he wrote it off as animals or simply the result of an active imagination given the circumstances. He went on to say that the investigators after him, and even the coroner noticed odd experiences in the home as well. Cold sensations. Phantom images. Typical indications of haunting.

I started to wonder if there was much more to the story of Old Man Ritter than the community was aware of. I drifted idly over his possessions on display while my mind explored the possibilities of a deeper story. I hovered over a photograph of a young man I could only assume was Ritter, as he stood smiling on a wooden porch with a young woman. I picked the photo up and inquired of the other two who the woman might be. Neither of them knew. Police records showed he had never been married, and had no siblings. The president agreed she had never known him to have a family. I set the picture back down, and that was when I noticed the journal.

Neither the constable nor the president took issue with me taking possession of Old Man Ritter's journal. There was no estate to be left to anyone, and his belongings were to be donated as per the will that he had left, which was found in his sock drawer. I had no idea what I expected to gain from the words I would find in his journal, and later that night when I returned home, I sat at the computer and began to write a short obituary for him. All the while, the journal sat beside me, beckoning me down the path of discovery. As soon as the obituary was complete, I settled into my recliner with my lamp on and opened the cover of the journal.

Just inside the book's leather cover was a short length of cord that tied in a small leather pouch. I squeezed the pouch in my fingers and felt a hard object within it. A trinket of some sort. Resting inside the book between the first page and the cover was another photograph of the same woman I saw in the photo at the funeral. She was older here, smiling in the center of the Polaroid portrait, and pregnant. On the back of the Polaroid was a name: Penny. I replaced the Polaroid and turned the first page.

Old Man Ritter's handwriting was quite good for a man, and his prose was talented. I wondered if, in another life, he could have made a fantastic author. The first entry in the journal was dated November 9th, 1941. He was fifteen years old, and his mother had gifted him the journal for his birthday. I was particularly fascinated with a passage he had placed in this entry. It was a piece of advice he claimed his mother gave him when he opened his present and discovered the leather journal.

*A man's story is all he has to give the world after he is gone, Franklin. Live a good story.*

I found the next entries in the journal no less riveting, and I poured through the pages of Old Man Ritter's life with abandon. He and his parents had come to Brightwood as immigrants from Europe, and they had homesteaded on the property he lived on. There were tales of hard winters, forest fires, financial depression, and the town as it grew around them. Ritter was a child full of life, and I had trouble associating the words of the boy I was reading with the legend of the man whose funeral I had attended. I could not fathom the energetic boy of those early pages growing up to become a silent hermit who died alone at the end of Ritter Road. Then, I reached a gap in entries, and everything changed.

In the Spring of 1944, shortly after Old Man Ritter had turned 18, news came that his father had been killed overseas in the war. His mother was beside herself, and her health quickly declined. Feeling helpless, Ritter had lied about his age and gone overseas to fight. Only a single entry was in the journal from this time, and it spoke of a town in Normandy that reminded Ritter of home. His unit had been pushing ahead with the offensive for days, and taken many losses. Ritter himself had been shot, and in the entry, he recounted a nurse he had met from Canada whom he developed a fancy towards. Her name was Penny. Unfortunately, during his recovery, his age was discovered and he was sent home before they could cultivate a romance.

Upon his arrival home, Old Man Ritter found his mother had died of illness. Alone and finding labour difficult due to his wounds, Ritter became a recluse. His journal entries spread out longer and longer as his life went on. He worked as a ghostwriter for a few publishing agencies, and some magazines and newspapers, but as technology developed, his interest waned. His military pension and royalties from his written works were more than enough to sustain his quaint lifestyle, and so his story went on.

As I finished the last entries in the journal, I felt a profound emptiness. The story of Old Man Ritter felt so hollow. Two pictures of the woman named Penny, one in which she was pregnant, but not a single mention of her past their chance encounter in Normandy? Was the horror of his short time at war, and the loss of his parents enough to quench the fire of life in the boy who wrote before the war? I slept very little that night. I was haunted by the mystery of this man.

The next morning, I called the local police detachment and asked to speak to the constable I had met at Old Man Ritter's funeral. He was surprised to hear from me, and even more so when I asked for access to the house at the end of Ritter Road. I could not give a solid reason for access, so I lied and told him I thought I may have found evidence of a next of kin. I told him about Penny, the photograph in the journal, and their encounter overseas during the war. It was enough to pique the constable's interest, and that afternoon I found myself driving up Ritter Road to meet the constable who was there waiting for me.

The constable refused to come inside with me, instead preferring to wait outside. I showed him the journal and the photo, he kept the book to peruse while I went inside the home. As I walked up the path leading to the home, I took note of the overgrown nature of the property and the lack of decorative landscaping. The home looked like a trapper cabin, with trees and wild plants growing almost right up to the walls. A path had been worn into the earth leading to a pair of steps onto a deck just large enough for a small table and single chair. The walls of the home were painted a dark green that almost looked like moss. Maybe it was. The front door was a well-kept oak with brass fittings and a half-moon glass window at its top. A single four-pane window looked into the home to the right of the door.

I looked back at the constable, who was now sitting inside his cruiser thumbing through the journal. Then I reached out and opened the front door. The inside of the home was a single space with no walls. A modest kitchen sat against the far wall on the right, with a fridge, an old propane stove, and a short run of countertop holding up a single sink. Clean dishes sat drying on a rack beside the sink. A single mattress bed with a metal bedframe sat opposite the room on the left, and a dresser leaned against the wall there also, serving double duty as a nightstand. Nothing adorned the top of the dresser now, but I imagined that to be where the framed photo of Ritter and Penny had been.

I stepped inside the room and looked directly to my left. I noticed then that the only door inside the whole house other than the front led to a tiny bathroom with a standup shower, toilet, and sink. Outside the bathroom in the main room was a wood fireplace and an old leather recliner. To my right inside the door was a kitchen table with two chairs.

In fairness, I had no idea what I was expecting to find as I entered Old Man Ritter's home. The minimalist nature of the cabin fit the reputation of the man perfectly. I walked around the room but found nothing. I understood what the constable had been saying though, about an odd sensation in the home. I felt it as I moved about. A general feeling of unease, like being watched. Cold spots in the air made the hair on my arms stand on end as I crossed the room towards the dresser.

As I reached the edge of the bed, I heard a creak in the floorboards unlike anywhere else I had stepped. A carpet under the bed covered some of the floor, placed in such a way as to prevent one's feet from touching the bare hardwood floor while sitting on the edge of the bed. I bent down and rolled up the edge of the carpet, noticing a latched part of the flooring with hinges. There was no lock, so I lifted the hatch open. As I did, something brushed by me, giving me a start. My eyes darted around the room but found only emptiness. I decided it must have been draft from the hatch, and peered into the hole in the floor.

A banker's box covered in dust lay beneath the floorboards under the hatch. Gently I reached in and lifted the box out. Sitting cross-legged on the floor, I set the box down and removed the lid. Inside the box was a horde of letters and more journals. With excitement, I began to sift through the letters, skimming over them and reading more into the mystery of who Old Man Ritter was.

Most of the letters I found were from a woman named Penny Barrett. It seemed Ritter had remained connected to her after all, only not in the way I had imagined. Penny had married an American soldier she met shortly after Ritter had been sent home. She had moved to Arkansas to live with him after the war, and they had a daughter together. Ritter was Penny's confidant and a lifelong pen-pal. Her husband had developed post-traumatic stress disorder after the war and dealt with it through alcohol and physical abuse. One of the last letters Ritter had received from Penny mentioned her finding the strength to leave him and come home to Canada. She had been planning to come to Ritter. In the box was a newspaper article from Arkansas. Penny never lived to escape her husband's wrath. Neither did their daughter. All had been killed in what the authorities called a murder-suicide.

My heart broke for Old Man Ritter as I read the letters and story of his life in that box under his bed.

More than once I thought I heard crying and looked around the room to confirm yet again that I was the sole occupant of the house. Letter by letter, piece by piece, the story of the man I had become fascinated with took shape. The world had taken everything from him, his family, his love, even his light. I thought back to that first entry in the journal of his mother's advice. *Live a good story.*

Had Franklin Aloysius Ritter lived a good story? It was hard for me to tell. At a very young age, he lost his father to a war that would eventually take his spirit and wound him for the rest of his days. He found love and came home to find he had lost the only remaining family he had. He pined and waited for a woman who was also taken from him. Senseless tragedy was all he seemed to ever know, at a time when there was not much help to be had for mental health. Especially for men. *Nice enough, but never spoke.*

After a long time of sitting in silence contemplating the haunted life of Old Man Ritter, I stood and picked up the box of letters and journals. I closed the hatch on the floor and replaced the carpet. Then I put the lid back on the banker's box and picked it up. As I crossed the room towards the front door, I felt the cold once more and stopped at the moment I did. I felt tremendous sadness in that moment, an almost overwhelming loneliness. A tear rolled down my cheek. At the front door, I stopped and turned back to the room.

"I'll tell your story" I whispered to the ghost in the house.

The next day I sat at my computer, the banker's box open on the floor beside me and the journal on my desk. As I watched the cursor blink on the first line of my new document, curiosity overcame me, and I lifted the journal in my hands. I slid open the drawstring on the leather pouch inside the journal and emptied the contents into my palm. A mushroomed bullet glinted in the light from my desk lamp. I knew it had to be the bullet that had injured him during the war, removed from the femur of his left thigh by surgeons overseas. The bullet that introduced him to Penny and changed his life. I smiled, set the bullet and the journal down, and began typing.

*The Haunting of Old Man Ritter; the story of Franklin Aloysius Ritter.*

The Dark Below the Ice and other stories

189

www.ingramcontent.com/pod-product-compliance
Lightning Source LLC
Chambersburg PA
CBHW030856200726
48289CB00003B/772